Secrets AND Scones

Secrets AND Scones

LAUREL REMINGTON

sourcebooks
jabberwocky

Copyright © 2018 by Laurel Remington
Cover and internal design © 2018 by Sourcebooks, Inc.
Cover design by Belle & Bird Design
Cover images © Kirsty Begg/Stocksy; master1305/Getty Images
Internal design by Danielle McNaughton/Sourcebooks, Inc.
Internal images © Freepik

Published by Sourcebooks Jabberwocky, an imprint of Sourcebooks, Inc.
P.O. Box 4410, Naperville, Illinois 60567-4410
(630) 961-3900
Fax: (630) 961-2168
sourcebooks.com

Originally published as *The Secret Cooking Club* in 2016 in the United Kingdom by Chicken House Ltd.

Library of Congress Cataloging-in-Publication Data

Names: Remington, Laurel, author.
Title: Secrets and scones : a secret recipe book / Laurel Remington.
Description: Naperville, Illinois : Sourcebooks Jabberwocky, [2018] |
    Summary: Scarlett, twelve, ended her friendships and activities when her
    mother started blogging about her every move, but when an elderly neighbor
    introduces her to cooking, she begins forging new connections.
Identifiers: LCCN 2018010649 | (pbk. : alk. paper)
Subjects: | CYAC: Middle schools--Fiction. | Schools--Fiction. | Mothers and
    daughters--Fiction. | Blogs--Fiction. | Cooking--Fiction. |
    Clubs--Fiction. | Fund raising--Fiction.
Classification: LCC PZ7.1.R462 Sec 2018 | DDC [Fic]--dc23 LC record available at
https://lccn.loc.gov/2018010649

Source of Production: Berryville Graphics, Inc., Berryville, Virginia, United States
Date of Production: September 2018
Run Number: 5013137

Printed and bound in the United States of America.
BVG 10 9 8 7 6 5 4 3 2 1

CHAPTER 1

The Worst Day of the Week

THE KETCHUP BOTTLE FARTS AND the last dregs sputter onto my sister's toast. My stomach twists, but to be honest, I was already feeling sick. It's Friday morning, 7:50 a.m.

Ten minutes to go.

"Is there any more, Scarlett?" Kelsie wipes her chin with the sleeve of her school shirt, leaving a sticky, red streak on the cuff.

"No," I say. "We're all out, and Mom forgot to order more. But you've got enough." I point to the lake of goop that's already smeared all over the toast—on top of the butter. Disgusting. Kelsie's almost seven, but she still eats everything with ketchup like it's some kind of fifth food group.

I push my soggy Wheaties around the bowl with the spoon,

but I can't eat. My classmates are probably bouncing off walls now that it's almost the weekend: texting their friends, packing for sleepovers, making cool plans. But not me. Right now, I wish a hole would open up in the center of our kitchen and swallow me.

Because at 8:00 a.m., Mom's blog post goes live.

My eyes dart frantically around the kitchen. Maybe I could stop it by shutting off the power, or "accidentally" dropping Mom's laptop in the bathtub, or becoming an amazing hacker and starting a virus that targets the computers of her thousands of followers—all in the next seven minutes. But I know it's too late. The new post is already on the server, hovering in cyber-space. Ready to pop into existence and broadcast the embarrassing details of my life to the world.

What will it be this week? I think back to everything I've done. Not much, since I quit all my clubs and activities at the end of last semester. That put a stop to posts like "Top Ten Reasons to Trash Your Kid's Violin" and "Tap-Dancing: Did I Give Birth to Three Left Feet?"

But even so, there's all the things I haven't done— like making sure Kelsie washes her hands after she uses the toilet and keeping my room clean. Two weeks ago, Mom did a "funny" little quiz about it: "Which Has More Germs: My

Daughter's Room or a Public Bathroom?" That one generated more than two hundred comments from her followers and got her five new advertisers for cleaning products on the site. That night, she ordered in a pizza so we could "celebrate." Kelsie ate my share (with ketchup), and I sat in my room wondering if it was ever going to end.

I give up on breakfast and take my bowl to the sink. The water runs upstairs, and I can hear Mom humming. She stayed up late putting the finishing touches on her post, and the fact that she's up early must mean it packs a punch. "Hurry up," I say to Kelsie. "I don't want to be late." Not that I ever want to show my face at school again, but better that than see Mom and pretend we're some kind of normal family.

"But I *need* more ketchup." Kelsie pouts at her plate. She scrapes her soggy bread and licks the ketchup off the knife.

"Look, I'll get some at the store after school, okay? Now go and put on your shoes."

I grab her plate and take it to the garbage can. On top of the overflowing trash are a few pieces of balled-up paper. I fish one out and uncrumple it. It's a printout of Mom's new post that went live—I check my watch—one minute ago. I look at the title: "Bye-Bye, Harvard: My Daughter Has No Interests."

The words blur on the page as my eyes swim with tears.

· CHAPTER 2 ·

The New Girl

I WALK KELSIE TO THE entrance of her school. A few of the moms whisper to one another when they see me. They've all read the new post. When I walk up the hill to my school, a boy from the soccer team makes a face at me. "Bye-bye, Harvard." He fakes a sob and a little wave.

The two boys he's walking with start laughing. "Hey, tell your mom we want another post about your underwear," one of them shouts.

"How about one on *your* underwear," I say, rolling my eyes. Because what else can I do other than play along with them? The day the post went up about the fact I still wore Disney Princess underwear was literally the most embarrassing of my life. Until the post "Did Something Die in That Gym

Bag?" went up. And the one on our talk about the "birds and the bees." My face is burning as I hurry off to my classroom. I know everyone at school has already read the latest post. There's nowhere to hide.

My first class is English. I take a seat at a table at the back, too flustered to realize that Gretchen is sitting right in front of me. She turns halfway around in her seat.

"Hi, Scarlett, you okay?" She sounds friendly, but I know it's all an act. Gretchen was one of the first girls to try to become "new best friends" with me when Mom's blog got popular. Back then, I'd thought it was cool that so many people wanted to be my NBF. But then I overheard Gretchen and Alison whispering together. Gretchen was saying how she wished her mom would write a blog about her, that it would be, like, *so* much more interesting than my mom's blog because she was running for student PTA representative, while I was the "most boring girl in the world." I'd cleared my throat so she'd known I was there. "Oh! Hi, Scarlett!" She'd recovered like the PTA princess she was. "How was your weekend?"

"Fine," I'd said then, but now I just shrug and say nothing. I don't ask how she is, because (a) I don't care, and (b) I don't want to hear about the student council, her new lavender bedroom furniture, her horseback-riding lessons, or any of the other things that Gretchen does because there's no one broadcasting her boring news to the world.

Alison doesn't even bother to be friendly. She ignores me, digging in her bag for her lip gloss. Alison's beautiful—tall and blond with perfect skin and big, green eyes—and what's more, she knows it. If she were Mom's daughter, there would be no boring news to broadcast. If I were Alison, I wouldn't have the time of day for people like me either.

Our English teacher, Ms. Carver, comes into the room and starts writing on the whiteboard. The bell rings, and at that moment someone runs past me up the aisle to an empty seat at the front of the room. It's Nick Farr, the cutest boy in the whole world. All the girls in my class think so.

"Nice of you to join us, Mr. Farr," Ms. Carver says, raising her eyebrows.

"My pleasure," Nick replies. He turns around in his seat and smirks at Alison. My insides droop like a wilting flower. Not that I want a boyfriend yet or anything, but never in a million years will boys like Nick notice that I even exist. And under the circumstances, that's probably a good thing. I'd die if anyone found out I liked him and it ended up in Mom's blog.

Because that's another thing I have to thank Gretchen for. I ignored the "most boring girl in the world" thing, and for a while, tried to make her like me. I worked on her PTA rep campaign, joined a few of the clubs she was in, helped her with her English homework, and tried really hard to be her friend.

But around then, Mom started blogging about more personal stuff, like that I bought deodorant with my allowance, that I still sleep with my old teddy bear, and that I was "trying to get in with the popular crowd." Things I'd never told Mom because I'd stopped talking to her by then. Someone was leaking stuff. I had my suspicions, so I told Gretchen some made-up things—just stupid stuff about wanting to dye my hair pink and get my nose pierced. Some of it showed up in Mom's blog. I was mortified—but not very surprised. I confronted Mom, but she managed to twist things around. She said that one of my friends was worried about me, and if I ever needed to talk she was there to listen… blah, blah, blah (and that maybe when I turned fourteen next year I could get my ears pierced). Whatever. So, that's when I quit all the clubs and activities, and stopped hanging out with Gretchen and Alison. I mean, why bother?

Ms. Carver begins class. My mind churns with thoughts about Mom and how I wish I could start a new life in a new town where no one knows me. Then maybe I could go back to being like I was before—a fun girl with lots of friends, eager to try new things, and laugh at myself when I made mistakes. Was

I really that girl only a little over two years ago? I can barely remember a time when I didn't have this gnawing shame in the pit of my stomach.

I'm staring straight ahead at the clock on the wall when I'm jarred back to reality by something Ms. Carver is saying: "It's never too early to start getting involved because it takes a lot more than good grades to get into a top college." I swallow hard. Of course—my teachers read it too.

Just then, the door to the classroom opens. Mrs. Franklin, the principal, walks in, followed by a girl I haven't seen before. There's something about her that makes me look twice. For one thing, she's really pretty—with black, shiny hair, a round-ish face, and bow-shaped lips that seem to naturally curve into a smile. But more than that, she looks like she might be nice. She glances at me for a second and our eyes meet.

"Sorry to interrupt," Mrs. Franklin says to our class. "This is Violet Sanders. She's new today, and she'll be joining you."

The principal gestures to the one empty seat—two away from mine—and the girl sits down. She takes out a notebook and pencil from her bag, biting her lip like she's a little nervous.

"Fine. Welcome, Violet." Ms. Carver shuffles her papers and goes back to the lesson.

The new girl stares straight ahead. I glance over at her.

Violet. I feel like we've got something in common because our names are both colors. But while my name seems all wrong—Scarlett is a name for a vibrant, outgoing, confident girl; not a dishwater blond, all elbows and knees, who'd rather hide in a bag than draw attention to herself—Violet's name is right for her. Even her eyes seem to be a bluish-purply color. It occurs to me that we might be friends—if she doesn't know who I am. It would be like starting fresh. But just then, Gretchen looks at Violet over her shoulder and smiles. The breath fizzles out of my chest. That's it, then. Violet will be claimed by the popular group, my secret will be revealed, and that will be that.

Which is exactly what happens. After class, Gretchen and Alison walk Violet out of the room shoulder to shoulder as though they've been best friends forever. They eat lunch together at the same table in the cafeteria. I watch them from across the room. Gretchen shows Violet something on her phone and points at me. Violet glances over, and I look away. Nick comes up to their table and sits down, and they all start talking and laughing.

At that point, I can't take it anymore. I get up, throw what's left of my tasteless beans and mystery-meat hot dog in the garbage, and hang out in the bathroom until the next class begins.

· CHAPTER 3 ·

A Bad Day for Somebody

BY THE END OF THE day, everyone at school has lost interest in the blog post, and I'm off the hook for another week. I walk home slowly, too exhausted to be embarrassed anymore. When I see Mom, I'll pretend that everything's fine, because if I don't, she'll blog about my "attitude" and how I don't appreciate the difficulties she faces.

Which is just so wrong. I kick hard at a rock in my way. I'm proud of Mom and what she's achieved. In less than three years, she's well on her way to becoming a really successful "Mommy Blogger." Each week, her followers log in to read her posts about the trials and tribulations of raising two children as a single mother after her husband ran off with his personal trainer. We hardly ever see Dad nowadays, and Mom refused to take any of his money from the moment he left—not even for me and Kelsie. She started her blog to support us. Which she's done.

Her proudest moment, at least as far as her followers are concerned, was when Dad came limping back a year or so ago, asking for a share of her blog money. She told him where to go in a vlog that went viral.

Now she writes her weekly post, and in between she has a lot of guest bloggers posting on her site, and a "Rant Page" for anyone to anonymously post on if they want to complain about their kids, husbands or partners, friends, work, mother-in-laws—whatever. She's got lots of advertisers and is even working on a deal with Superdrug, a drugstore chain, to make a Mom Survival Kit that they'll sell in all their stores.

So, it's cool she's an online celebrity, and while we're not rich or anything, she's made enough money for us to move into a three-bedroom house where I get my own room and don't have to share with my sister. But there's one big problem: Her trials and tribulations, rants, and things she has to "survive" mostly involve me, and sometimes Kelsie. I know she loves us, but sometimes I think she must really hate being a mom.

I walk slower and slower the closer I get to home. The thought of another evening spent watching *Full House* reruns with Kelsie makes me feel like a rag doll with the stuffing knocked out. I wonder what Violet is doing tonight. Probably spending a nice evening with her parents, telling them about her first day at school and the cool new friends she's made, then settling down to play a board game or practice piano or learn Chinese or something—

As I turn down my street, my heart jumps to my throat. An ambulance with flashing lights is parked at the end of the block, right in front of our house. Two paramedics are loading a stretcher inside. Mom once told me that "it's a bad day for somebody" whenever there's an ambulance or the police come over.

I start to run, my backpack banging up and down on my back. Is it Mom? Kelsie? As the red and white lights blink on and off, all the mean thoughts I've ever had about them flash before my eyes. I wish I could unthink them.

The paramedic shuts the ambulance door. I realize they're actually in front of the house next door. An old woman named Mrs. Simpson lives there. I've never met her, and I only know her name because a deliveryman who was looking for her house came to ours by mistake. Her house is kind of spooky—the curtains are always closed and I've never seen a light on. When we moved here a few months ago, Mom talked about inviting her over for coffee, but surprise, surprise, it never happened.

I walk up to the paramedic. "Is Mrs. Simpson okay?"

"She'll be fine. She had a little fall," he says. "Got a bump on the head. She managed to dial nine-one-one, otherwise…" He shakes his head. "You a relative?"

"No. I don't really know her."

He climbs into the passenger seat. "Okay, well, she's in good hands now; we'll take it from here."

The ambulance pulls away, and the siren begins to wail. I stand alone on the sidewalk, watching until it disappears around the corner. In the other houses down the street, there's not even a curtain twitching in a downstairs window. No one seems to have noticed anything.

Inside our house, Kelsie's watching TV in the living room. I plunk down my bag and go to the kitchen. The door to Mom's office—the "Mom Cave"—is open.

"Scarlett? Is that you?" she calls out.

"Yeah," I say. Anger simmers in my chest. Mom has so many thousands of online "friends," but has never paid the slightest bit of attention to the old woman next door. Not that I have either. And now it might be too late.

"Guess what?" Mom rushes out of her office like a

slightly wrinkled tornado. She embraces me in a hug. For a second I almost give in to the comforting feeling and hug her back. But all too quickly, the other stuff comes rushing too. I pull away.

"What?" I say cautiously.

"I'm in Superdrug! They signed the contract today. They're going to stock the survival kit in two hundred stores to start with. Isn't that fantastic?"

"Um, yeah."

"Here, let me show you the prototype." She goes to the counter and picks up a little box printed with purple and pink. "We've got some hand lotion and sanitizer, a gel face mask, earplugs, lip balm, jelly beans, and a hollow chocolate egg with a *Mom Survival Tip* inside."

"Oh."

"They wouldn't let me include the caffeine pills, but we're going to add a coffee sachet. You know, like a tea bag?"

"Great. Didn't you hear the ambulance?"

"What ambulance? Anyway, I've still got to choose the jelly bean colors. What do you think about pink?"

"Pink's good." Or *scarlet*...I don't add.

"Terrific. Pink it is. I'll email them now." She heads for the door of her office.

"Mrs. Simpson had a fall," I say. "They took her to the hospital."

"Who?" She barely pauses.

"The neighbor next door. The old woman."

"Oh, is that her name?"

"Yeah."

"Well…too bad." She gives a little shrug. "Oh, and Scarlett, would you mind getting Kelsie her juice? I've got to prepare for tonight's online chat. It's on how to talk to your teenager."

"Sure," I say through my teeth.

"Thanks. Oh, and one more thing…"

"Yeah?"

"Thanks for being such a big help."

She closes the door, and I stare for a moment at the Mom Cave sign swinging on its hook. Part of me wants to throw open the door and demand that she "talk to her teenager" for real. I'd tell her exactly how I feel, tell her exactly how bad my day has been thanks to her, and tell her exactly where she, her two hundred Superdrug stores, and her thousands of online followers can go. But to be honest, it's just not worth it. Much better to simply check off my tasks one by one—dinner, homework, watching TV, shower—and go to bed.

Which is exactly what I do. By the end of the evening, my

anger has dulled, and I start to feel numb. I collapse on my bed more tired from doing nothing than if I'd run a marathon. And then I can't sleep. I think about Mrs. Simpson. It's been a bad day for her—much worse than for me. I hope she's okay. I close my eyes and try to think good thoughts for her, but my mind keeps wandering. And then, just as I'm finally starting to drift off, I'm startled awake by an earsplitting screech.

· CHAPTER 4 ·

A Noise
in the Night

I JOLT UPRIGHT IN THE circle of light from my lamp. That sound: It was like someone—or something—is being tortured. And it came from the other side of the wall that separates our house from Mrs. Simpson's. Panic floods through me. She must have come home from the hospital and hurt herself again. Maybe this time she won't be able to get to the phone. Maybe this time she'll die and it will be my fault. And the headline of OLD WOMAN LEFT TO DIE AS GIRL IGNORES CRY FOR HELP will be in all the newspapers, not just on Mom's blog.

I swing out of bed and tiptoe into the hallway. My sister's room is dark, and I can hear her breathing. There's a crack of light below Mom's door and the sound of typing. For a second I think of knocking. But she'll just tell me it's nothing and send me back to bed.

Sneaking downstairs to the kitchen, I grab a flashlight from the drawer by the sink. The door to the backyard squeaks when I open it and, holding my breath, step outside. The moon is a perfect crescent, and there are one or two stars twinkling among wispy clouds. I stand on a bucket and look over the fence. Nothing seems out of the ordinary. The back of Mrs. Simpson's house is dark.

I return to our house and tiptoe out the front door. Everything is silent in the street. A thin coat of dew has formed on the windshields of the cars, the tiny droplets glittering in the moonlight. I go around the hedge that separates our house from Mrs. Simpson's. Her door is black and glossy with a brass mailbox and knocker. As I lift my hand to knock, I hear it again—the bone-chilling wail from inside.

I forget all about knocking and turn the door handle. But it's locked. My heart thunders as I switch on the flashlight. There's an old flowerpot next to the door, and I check underneath it. Nothing. I look under the recycling container and, finally, under the doormat. A gold key shines in the circle of light. I mean, who actually leaves their key under the mat? I fumble with the key in the lock and push open the door.

The house is pitch-black and silent and smells of dusty curtains and Ivory soap. I flick the flashlight around the room, scared I might see a body lying in a pool of blood. Instead, there's some dark, clunky furniture, a sagging sofa and chairs, and lots of knickknacks. The room says *old lady*. I shine the flashlight toward the door at the back of the room that must lead to the kitchen, and then I'm the one who yelps.

Eyes. Yellow and unfriendly. I'm so jumpy it takes me a second to realize it's not a monster or a ghost, but a cat—pure black with a white collar around its neck.

"Oh, you scared me!" I say. And a second later, I realize how stupid I've been. "It was you, wasn't it, doing all that screeching?"

The cat swishes its long, fluffy tail, still looking as though some kind of demon in animal form. It takes a few steps toward me, holding its head proudly in the air. My skin tickles as it rubs against my bare legs and starts to purr.

"You're lonely, is that it?" I reach down and pick up the cat. It nestles into my arms, staring at me with big eyes that now seem more sad than frightening. "And hungry, maybe?"

The cat rubs its cheek against mine.

I've never had a cat—or any kind of pet—but I instinctively snuggle it closer in my arms like some kind of lost, kindred spirit.

"Those paramedics must have locked you out of the kitchen. Let's see if we can find you some food."

The cat squirms in my arms, and I put it down. It hurries over to a door that in our house leads to the dining room, and starts to meow. I open the door and switch on the light.

What I see makes me gasp.

· CHAPTER 5 ·

Rosemary's Kitchen

THE KITCHEN IS AMAZING—THAT'S the only word for it. It's enormous, with a high, beamed ceiling and a spotless floor. Every surface sparkles: shiny stainless steel, polished wood, mirror-black granite. Copper pots hang from a rack on the ceiling, and there's an entire wall of cookbooks. In one corner is a giant oven, next to a double-wide fridge, and a glass cupboard filled with just about every kind of kitchen gadget. A wooden table takes up the entire back of the room, and there's a fireplace big enough to stand up in. The whole thing seems like heaven for a cook—and anyone around to eat the food. I breathe in the smell of spices and fresh lemon and smile. I can't believe all this is here, just on the other side of the wall from the three rooms that make up our cramped little kitchen, dining/junk room, and the Mom Cave.

The cat meanders over to an empty bowl next to the oven. It looks at me with its big, yellow eyes and begins to meow. Walking in, I go over to the fridge. A magnetic sign on the door says ROSEMARY'S KITCHEN. Inside, it's stocked with practically a whole supermarket's worth of fresh food. I take out a carton of organic milk and an open can of tuna-flavored cat food. "I guess Mrs. Simpson's name must be Rosemary," I say, emptying the milk and cat food into bowls. "I didn't know."

The cat swishes its tail and dives into the food. I continue looking around. I'm immediately drawn to the shelves of cookbooks—one whole shelf is dedicated to a series of books called *Encyclopedia of Herbs and Spices*. The shelf at eye level has three different cookbooks by Mrs. Beeton, plus a few big-name celebrity cookbooks: Ina Garten, Jamie Oliver, Mary Berry. Most of them look almost new. There are some well-used books by authors I don't recognize, including Elizabeth David, Julia Child, and Auguste Escoffier. But what interests me the most is the top shelf. It has an assortment of very old-looking books in different colors, shapes, and sizes. I grab one that catches my eye: *Recipes Passed Down from Mother to Daughter*. It's got a drawing of a pretty 1950s mom on the cover, giving her apple-cheeked daughter some biscuits fresh out of the oven. Somehow I'm pretty sure it won't have an entry for "frozen fish sticks and tater tots" which is the only recipe my mom's "passed down" to me.

I put it back on the shelf. Behind me, the cat is purring and eating at the same time. I turn around and something on the kitchen counter catches my eye. Propped open on a wooden book stand is a notebook bound in tattered red cloth, the front marbled in red, green, and blue. It must be really old. Curious to see what Mrs. Simpson was cooking before her accident, I pick it up. The book feels oddly warm in my hands, like a fresh-baked loaf of bread. I open the cover. On the first page is a note, loopy letters handwritten in black ink:

To my little cook—May you find the secret ingredient.

I read the words out loud to the cat, wondering who the "little cook" is, and whether she—or he—found the secret ingredient. The cat swishes its tail, quite content with the food in its bowl.

I flip through the notebook. There are a bunch of recipes written out in pen, with a few notes and crossings-out, but there are also pictures—some done in pencil and crayon, others cut out of magazines and old newspapers and glued to the page—of cakes, pies, bread, meat, and other foods. There's also a whole section of recipes based on nursery rhymes with little poems and stories including "Hansel and Gretel" written out in fancy lettering. It must have taken so much time to collect and write out the recipes and all the little rhymes and illustrations—years maybe. How lucky the little cook must have been to have someone care so much. I don't know anything about cooking, but as I hold the recipe book in my hands, I have a funny feeling the book is special somehow.

I close the notebook. The cat has finished its tuna and begins lapping up the milk like an after-dinner coffee. Then it carefully licks its whiskers. Swishing its tail, it walks slowly out of the kitchen. I turn the light off and follow it to the living room. It jumps on to one of the threadbare chairs.

"You're welcome," I say, somewhat touchy. "And I guess you'll be expecting me to come back tomorrow to feed you again?"

The cat curls up into a ball, snuggling its face into its wispy black tail. Its purrs grow slower, and soon it's fast asleep.

I move silently to the front door and shut off the flashlight so no one will see me. I slip out of Mrs. Simpson's house and put the key under the mat, with the handwritten recipe book still tucked under my arm.

· CHAPTER 6 ·

The Little Recipe Book

I DON'T REALLY KNOW WHY I took the notebook from Mrs. Simpson's kitchen. It's not as though I'm actually going to *cook* anything at home. I can just picture Mom rubbing her hands with glee if I did: "Help, My Daughter Is Trying to Poison Me/Burn Down the House/Make Me Throw Up During My Marketing Meeting." I stick the recipe book under my pillow. Part of the reason I keep my room—according to one of Mom's blog posts—"like a toxic waste dump" is so she won't ever go in there.

Downstairs the next morning, Mom is pacing around the kitchen, taking two minutes out of her busy day to drink a cup of instant coffee.

"So, do you have any plans for the weekend, Scarlett?" Mom says.

"Um…" My brain furiously calculates the probabilities of providing her with blog material, depending on whether I say yes or no. I settle on: "Not really, but I've got some homework to do."

"Kelsie went to a birthday party this morning, and I've got a guest blog post to write. Can you go over to Stacie's house?"

"She's visiting her grandma," I lie. Stacie was my best friend last year, before the whole Gretchen and Alison thing. Then Mom wrote a post called "Psst…Want to Know a Secret? My Daughter's Best Friend Is Really Dull." And then, big surprise, Stacie stopped speaking to me and dropped me as a friend. Luckily, she goes to a private school, so I don't have to see her every day.

"That's nice." Mom puts down the coffee cup and digs around in the fridge. She takes out a piece of cold pizza and nibbles on it. "And how's school? You joining any new clubs?"

"No, Mom." I take a box of cereal from the top of the fridge and pour some into a bowl. Then I sit and stare at it.

Mom shakes her head and *tsk*s. "I just don't know what's up with you, Scarlett. When I was your age, I had lots of friends. Plus, I did swimming and basketball and…"

I stop listening. Mom's already written a sappy blog post called "I Really Was Your Age Once..." where she went on about the days before cell phones, iPads, and Snapchat, when she and her friends passed notes in class and gossiped about boys. That post alone got more than three hundred and fifty sympathetic comments from her followers. She won't write another one that's too similar, so I'm off the hook.

"Yeah, Mom, I know. But I'm sure Harvard can live without me." I force myself to take a bite of the cereal. It tastes like soggy cardboard.

Mom frowns. "Well, if you're not doing anything, maybe you can pick up a few things for me at the store."

"Sure, whatever." I take my bowl to the sink.

"You didn't eat any of that cereal." Mom's eyes sharpen. "Is something wrong?"

"No." I pause for a second. "I'm not hungry."

She cocks her head. "You're not anorexic, are you?"

"No, Mom. The cereal's a little stale."

"Oh." She tosses the pizza crust in the garbage and puts the kettle back on to boil. When she's not looking, I take the crust out of the trash and put it in the compost bucket instead.

"Okay, Scarlett, whatever you say." Mom glances at me over her shoulder. "But you're a teenager now. You need to keep your blood sugar up." I can almost see the gears in her brain working overtime: "Does My Daughter Have an Eating Disorder, or Is She Just Obstinate?"

"Whatever, Mom. I'll have a snack later."

I go up to my room and take out the little recipe book from under my pillow. I open it and reread the inscription inside the cover: *To my little cook— May you find the secret ingredient.*

I wonder what it was like for the little cook—a daughter or son, I assume—to spend time with their mom learning how to bake and cook wonderful dishes. One thing's for sure, I can't imagine *my* mom ever doing something like that with me.

I flip through the nursery rhyme section of the notebook, smiling at the recipes for pies, bread, and gingerbread, and the little rhymes about "The Cat and the Fiddle" and "Goosey, Goosey Gander." There are a few recipes for basic things: Humpty Dumpty's Perfect Eggs and Yankee Doodle's Four-Cheese Macaroni. There's also an ABC of Spices, most of which I've never heard of. But lots of the ingredients make my mouth water: buttercream, ginger, molasses, cocoa, and powdered sugar. Best of all are the cinnamon scones. There's a picture done in pen and colored in with crayon of little, fluffy triangles steaming hot in a basket with a red-and-white gingham cloth. My stomach growls just thinking about them. If I could try one recipe, it would be that.

But I can't try any of the recipes. Not here at home where Mom would know about it.

So, I'll have to find another way.

· CHAPTER 7 ·

The House Next Door

THE STREET IS QUIET AS I slip out the front door. I walk up the weedy stone path to Mrs. Simpson's house. I tell myself that it's not really breaking and entering when there's an old woman in the hospital and a cat that needs feeding. And a recipe book that needs returning. It's a no-brainer, really. And if, by some chance, Mrs. Simpson is already home from the hospital, I'll tell her I came over to look after the cat.

No one answers when I knock on the door. The key is still under the mat. With a quick glance around to make sure no one's watching, I let myself into Mrs. Simpson's house.

The first thing I see are those two yellow eyes again, shining like twin moons. The cat meows impatiently as if it's been waiting for me and I'm late. "Hi," I say. "You still here by yourself?" The cat swishes its tail. It gets to its feet and leads the way to the kitchen.

I get down to business—scoping out where everything is so I can get on with my plan. Just being here again has made up my mind. I've found a special little recipe book and the perfect kitchen. And now...

I'm going to cook something.

One by one, I open the cupboards. It's like exploring a supermarket baking aisle. There are dozens of little jars and cans of herbs and spices. There are bags of flour: stone-ground, buckwheat, spelt, malted wheat grain; and sugars: demerara, powdered, icing, muscovado—who knew there were so many different kinds? Even though everything is labeled, it's still kind of overwhelming. The cat rubs against my leg and stands in front of one of the cupboards.

"Okay, okay, I get it. You're hungry again." I open the cupboard and find a large supply of cat food. I dig around some more until I spot a can opener in a drawer, along with a complete set of baking utensils and electric appliances, most of which I have no idea what to do with, and some of which look like scary dentist instruments.

Once the cat has its head contentedly in its bowl, I take out the little recipe book and set it on the book stand.

It practically falls open to the recipe for cinnamon scones. I read over the instructions: Mix everything together, then roll out the dough, and cut out little triangle shapes that are to be dusted with more cinnamon and sugar. Then they're supposed to rise and become all fluffy in the oven. It sounds straightforward enough, but suddenly I feel nervous.

What business do I have breaking and entering and using Mrs. Simpson's things? And worse, what makes me think I can possibly bake anything? I've never really tried before, except once. I wanted to surprise Mom with a cake for her birthday, so I bought a cake mix at the corner store. It turned out I didn't have enough eggs, and the butter was as hard as a rock. The mixture ended up all powdery and lumpy. Then I left it in the oven too long, and it came out charred and smoky. I threw it in the trash before Mom even knew I'd tried.

I take a deep breath. I'm here now, so I may as well give it a try. Most of the ingredients I need—flour, butter, baking powder, salt—are already sitting on the counter, along with a jar of Ceylon cinnamon. Strange that I didn't notice them last night. It's as if Mrs. Simpson had been getting ready to bake scones. It makes me feel a little creepy, almost like she's here with me in the kitchen, looking over my shoulder, making sure I do it right. I peek quickly behind me. There's no one there.

"Silly," I say out loud. Everything seems normal again. Finished eating, the cat curls up in its basket next to the oven and begins licking its paws. I wash my hands and grab a rose-patterned apron from a hook by the fridge. Before I can lose my nerve, I put it over my head and tie it around my waist. I'm ready.

I've never been one of those kids who liked playing in the sand, making mud pies, finger painting, or generally making messes. So, that might be why I had never guessed how satisfying it could be to measure out ingredients, put them into a bowl, then stir them together. Peering out of its basket, the cat keeps an eye on my progress.

At first the mixture is lumpy and dry, and all my worries come back that I've done something wrong. I think about adding more milk, but I decide, just this once, to trust the recipe. I keep on stirring. The smell of cinnamon goes to my head, and for some reason I feel happier and calmer than I have in a long time. When the dough is a soft mass in the bowl, I sprinkle some flour on the counter to start rolling it out.

But before I can work on the dough, disaster strikes. The doorbell rings, and then a key turns in the lock.

· CHAPTER 8 ·

A Taste of Cinnamon

SOMEONE'S HERE! PANICKING, I LOOK around. I could run out the back door, but I'd be trapped in the backyard, and besides, the kitchen's a mess and it's obvious what I've been doing. The cat jumps up from its basket as if it's trying to figure out how to cover for me. I pull off the apron and start trying to clean up—for all the good it's going to do. And then I hear a woman's voice: "Look, I'm sorry if you're bored, but I have to do this. You said you wanted to come. Next time, stay at home."

I don't hear a reply because the front door closes and something—a purse maybe?—thumps to the floor. Then there's the sound of heels clicking in the hallway. I look around for a place to hide—the broom closet? The fireplace? Inside the oven?

The knob on the door turns. I stand there paralyzed, my

heart thundering. The cat comes up beside me, the fur on its back standing up. The door opens. I come face-to-face with just about the last person I was expecting to see…

Violet.

"Oh, you scared me!" Her hands fly to her mouth. "I…I didn't know anyone was here."

"Um, yeah." I smile through my teeth. "I was just…just—"

"Violet? Is there someone in there?"

Frantically, I gesture at the cat.

"No, Aunt Hilda. Just a cat." Violet gives a fake-sounding sneeze for effect.

"All right," Aunt Hilda says. "I'm going to start with the upstairs. Don't touch anything, okay?"

"Okay."

The high heels click up the stairs.

"Thanks for that," I say. My heart slows to a fast jog.

"What are you doing here?" She eyes the kitchen and the mess I've made.

"I was making scones," I say sheepishly. "Cinnamon."

She sniffs the air. "It smells good in here. Not cinnamon, though, but something else?"

"I don't know—butter maybe? Or the dough? But dough doesn't really smell like anything, does it?"

"It's nice." She smiles. "But you don't live here, right? My aunt said the house belongs to some old woman."

"Mrs. Simpson," I say. "Rosemary. She's a neighbor. We live next door."

"Oh. It's cool that she lets you use her kitchen."

"Yeah…it is."

"Violet?" The aunt's voice comes closer. "Did you say something?"

"No, Aunt Hilda," Violet calls out.

"Okay, but I need to see the…"

The aunt appears at the kitchen door, the clicking of her heels coming to an abrupt stop. She's about Mom's age but much taller in her heels, and she has the same blue-black hair as Violet. She's wearing a stylish gray suit and a floral scarf.

"…kitchen," she trails off, her mouth gaping open. "Wow," she says. "It's…big." She glances around. "What a fantastic space. And look at the oven—it's enormous." She gestures toward the cast-iron oven that's as big as a small car. It was a double-wide with several stoves and hot plates.

"It's huge," I agree.

Her eyes come to rest on me. "And who are you?"

"I'm Scarlett. From next door. I…uh, came over to feed the cat."

"Looks like you're feeding yourself too." Frowning, she gestures at the mess of flour and dry ingredients sprinkled on the counter and the floor. "If you're here without permission, then you'd better be gone when Mr. Kruffs arrives."

"Mr. Kruffs?" The name sounds vaguely familiar. "Who's he?"

Violet's aunt sizes me up as if she's debating whether to answer. "Emory Kruffs. He's running for city council." She wanders over and examines the oven. "You may have seen his name on posters."

"Maybe."

"I'm a real estate agent. He's arranged for me to give him an assessment of the house. He's supposed to meet me here."

"Is it his house?" I ask.

"Well." She frowns. "Not exactly. I think he's the nephew of the owner."

"Rosemary Simpson," I say. "She's the woman who lives here. Do you know if she's okay?"

She shrugs. "No idea. Sorry."

"Well, someone needs to feed the cat until she gets back," I say firmly. "I mean, I'm sure Mrs. Simpson wouldn't want it to starve. And I live right next door."

"The cat…" she muses. "I see your point, but if Mr.

Kruffs sees this mess, then I don't know. I wouldn't let him catch you here—"

"I was just leaving," I say. "That is, after I cut out the scones and put them in the oven." I wince. "And, you know… um…take them out again. Is that okay?"

"Cool," Violet says. "Can I watch?" She looks doubtfully at her aunt.

Something beeps loudly, startling us all. A text message. Aunt Hilda takes out her phone and stares at the screen. "This must be your lucky day," she says. "Mr. Kruffs just canceled our meeting."

Violet and I look at each other and grin.

Aunt Hilda checks the time. "I'm going to finish looking around and draft the email for the assessment," she says. "You two had better make sure this kitchen is spotless when you're done." Her heels click away to the front room where she switches on a table lamp.

I turn to Violet. "Thanks for staying," I say. "I mean, it was kind of creepy being here by myself. Especially if that Mr. Kruffs had turned up."

"No problem," Violet says. "It's not like I've got anything better to do. And I've always liked scones—that is, if you're sharing." Her smile grows wider.

"I'll think about it." I laugh. We both look into the bowl of

mixed-up dough. I breathe in deeply. It smells delicious and...
doughy. I put the soft ball on the counter and gently roll it out.
The rolling pin sticks a little to the dough, so I sprinkle more
flour over it, trying to look as though I know what I'm doing.

"Did your mom teach you how to cook?" Violet sounds
almost impressed.

"No." My mind whirls, trying to think of something cool—
like my grandma was a *Cake Wars* finalist—or anything like
that. But I don't want to lie to Violet. I point to the recipe book.
"Actually, I've never made scones before," I say. "I'm teaching
myself." Flustered, I turn away from her and concentrate on
cutting the dough into little triangle shapes. I check the recipe
again and sprinkle a sweet-smelling mixture of cinnamon and
sugar on the tops.

"You're kidding." Violet giggles in amazement. "You have
cooked before, though, right?"

I stand a little straighter. "Well, I guess I have. I can make
a grilled cheese sandwich. Does that count?"

"Yes, it does! I can't even make toast without burning it."

"Well, I can barely even plug in the toaster!"

We look at each other and both start laughing. It's not as if
it's really *that* funny, but I'm so out of practice my side begins
to hurt. I get the idea that maybe it's the same for her.

Violet helps me cut out the rest of the scones, and we put them on a buttered baking tray. As we work, I tell her about the ambulance taking Mrs. Simpson away, and about the cat, and how I broke into the house and found the recipe book and the kitchen. "I had no idea it was here," I say. "Right on the other side of our house."

"It's awesome," Violet says. She picks up the recipe book and flips through it. "And this book—I can't believe someone took the time to write all this out by hand."

"Yeah," I say. "I wonder who the little cook was."

Violet reads the inscription inside the cover. "And the secret ingredient… What's that?"

"I don't know."

She goes back to the page with the scone recipe. "Well, I can see why you wanted to try making these scones," she says. "They look so delicious."

"Yeah." My brow furrows in concentration. We've cut out all the, scones and I can't put off any longer the thing I've been dreading—tackling the oven.

"Ever used one of these things before?" I ask futilely.

"I don't think I've ever even seen one." We both burst out laughing again. She helps me carry the trays over.

I look inside one of the cast-iron doors. Luckily, there are some wire racks—it looks like a normal oven once you open it. "Look," Violet says, "there's a temperature dial. What should I put it on?"

I put the trays down and check the recipe in the notebook. "Put it on four hundred degrees." I decide not to spoil the moment by mentioning we were supposed to preheat the oven. Oh well. "They should be ready in about twenty minutes."

"I can't wait to try one," Violet says.

My stomach growls in agreement.

· CHAPTER 9 ·

The Scent of Childhood

WHEN I GET HOME, I'M surprised to see Mom sitting at the table helping Kelsie read her phonics book. "Where have you been?" she asks me without looking up. "No, Kels, there's an *l*—it's 'pool,' not 'poop.'"

"I went to the library to do some homework."

"Oh." She sounds disappointed. There's very little blogging material in me going to the library, but I'm sure that my sister's "pool" versus "poop" confusion will figure prominently in the next post. "Well, next time let me know, okay?"

"Okay."

"And I hope you're hungry because I made baked macaroni and cheese. It's on top of the stove."

"Really?" I raise an eyebrow. Even though I'm completely stuffed with the most delicious, fluffy cinnamon scones I could ever imagine eating—let alone making myself—I feel kind of bummed I missed what, in our house at least, passes for a real meal.

"I'll have a little," I say. "Sorry, I didn't know you were cooking."

"I wasn't going to." She leans forward on her elbows. "I mean, *me*? Cook?" She gives a little laugh. "But it was the oddest thing…"

"What?"

"I was in my office, and there was this smell." Her brow furrows. "Some kind of spice—cinnamon, maybe. It reminded me of something. I don't know what really. Something from my childhood."

"Your childhood?" I try not to sound surprised. One thing Mom never talks or blogs about is her childhood, before she got to her teenage years anyway. Sometimes I wonder if she was ever my age.

She shrugs. "I guess a neighbor must have been cooking. It was as if I was back in my grandma's kitchen. They do say that smell is one of the strongest senses for triggering memories." She stares at the oven for a second.

"That's interesting," I say. "What was your grandma like? You never really talk about her."

She blinks quickly. "Oh, I don't know." She waves away my question. "I guess my nose is just extra sensitive today. You'd think I was pregnant or something." She stands and puts the kettle on, twisting her hands in what I recognize as her *I've just thought of something to blog about* way. "I mean, when I was pregnant with you girls, I was throwing up left and right. For all nine months of it, each time. Everything tasted like salt and"—she laughs—"seemed to smell like dog poop!"

"Mommy, you said poop!" Kelsie says triumphantly.

"Oops, I meant 'pool' of course!" Mom points back to the book, and she and Kelsie both giggle. Even I have to smile, though we are all *far* too old for that kind of joke. I serve myself a small bowl of macaroni and cheese, mulling over what Mom said about how she could smell the cooking through the wall. It's kind of odd she's never mentioned it before. I mean, before her accident, Mrs. Simpson must have cooked all the time.

I sit at the table with the bowl and take a bite. I'm so surprised I almost choke. "It's *good*, Mom," I say.

"I made the sauce myself."

"You did?"

She narrows her eyes. "Don't look so surprised. Believe it or not, Scarlett, not everything is made in the microwave."

Later that night, as I'm lying on my bed staring at the glow-in-the-dark stars on my ceiling, I think about everything that's happened over the last two days—from the yowling cat, to the kitchen and cookbook—from meeting Violet unexpectedly, to Mom's homemade cheese sauce.

Most of all, though, I think about making the scones. My mouth waters as I remember their comforting doughy taste. Because I hadn't preheated the oven, we left them in for much longer than they should have needed. I was kind of worried they would be burnt. But when we took them out, they were nice and golden brown on the bottom. To me, they tasted perfect.

They looked perfect too—Violet even snapped a few pics of them on her phone.

She and I each ate two, and Violet's aunt ate one. I wrapped the rest up and stored them in a plastic container; they're still downstairs in my bag, fourteen of them. I feel a little bit mean for not sharing them with Kelsie and Mom, but I don't want to explain where they came from.

When I hear Mom's bedroom door close, I tiptoe downstairs, unwrap the scones, and leave two of them out on a plate on the kitchen table. Let Mom and her followers try to figure out who made them. She'll never guess in a million years it was her boring daughter. I climb back in my bed and drift off to sleep, still breathing in the phantom smell of cinnamon.

CHAPTER 10

A Dollop of Tears

THE NEXT MORNING, THE SCONES are gone (with a plate of crumbs left behind on the table), and the door to the Mom Cave is shut.

The day goes slowly—the usual kind of Sunday: Mom working, me playing with Kelsie until Mom comes out and zaps dinner in the microwave, then falls asleep on the sofa. I creep into Mrs. Simpson's house just before dinner to feed her cat, but I feel uneasy there by myself. What if her nephew comes by today after Violet's aunt talks to him? I sneak out again, wondering if I'll ever have the courage to go back there and use the kitchen. Or will the scones be our first and last attempt?

The next morning, Mom is up and in her office by the

time I come downstairs. I can hear her voice, talking animatedly to someone on her phone. When I'm ready to leave for school and have gotten Kelsie ready too, Mom still hasn't emerged. I feel kind of sad that she hasn't even bothered to come out to say goodbye to us. But when I pick up my backpack (filled with a dozen scones) and leave the house, I feel better.

Before class is about to begin, Violet comes up to me in the hall. "Do you have them?" she whispers behind her hand. I feel a little flicker of pride when I see that, behind her, Gretchen and Alison are looking in our direction.

"Yeah," I say. "I gave one—well, two, actually—to Mom. But I've got the rest with me. Do you want one?"

"Later." Violet smiles conspiratorially. "In fact, I have an idea."

"What?"

"You'll see. Leave them with me. And come to the cafeteria at lunchtime, okay?"

I ignore a tiny stab of alarm. "Okay."

There are worry knots in my chest later as I walk into the cafeteria. On a table at the center is a large pink-and-purple

Easter basket. I watch as a few kids go up to it and look inside. There's a sign taped to the handle of the basket.

FREE SAMPLES!

My stomach clenches. I sit at a table near the door and watch the steady stream of people going up to the basket and helping themselves. A moment later, Violet plunks down beside me.

"Do you like my surprise?" she whispers. "I set it up without the cafeteria workers seeing me."

I stand up awkwardly. "Um...I'll see you later, okay? I've got to see Ms. Carver about an essay I wrote."

Violet stops smiling. "What's up with you?"

"Nothing." My voice catches. "You didn't tell anyone I helped make the scones, did you?"

"No, I didn't. But what's the problem? Everybody loves them."

I look over to the central table. People are hovering around like wasps at a picnic. Some kids are talking to other kids that I know for sure aren't their friends. The volume of noise in the room rises steadily. There were only twelve scones, but people seem to be sharing them—even the crumbs.

"Yeah, great. It's just…could you not mention my name? I mean, can you say that you made them?"

Violet puts her hands on her hips. "For your information, no one saw me put them there. I thought it would be fun to have it be a secret. I'm not going to say who made them."

"Oh." I feel so stupid. I can't tell Violet about why I don't want to be involved. It all just sounds so dorky.

"So, what's wrong, Scarlett?"

"Nothing." I turn away and leave the cafeteria.

I rush down the hallway. Violet could have been my friend and I've ruined it. Why can't I just tell her the truth—that I'm scared to do anything because of Mom and her stupid blog? Why did I go to Mrs. Simpson's house, and why did Violet have to find me? Why did Violet have to come to our school at all?

In the girls' bathroom, I practically slam into Gretchen and Alison, who are on their way out. "Hey, watch it." Gretchen teeters backward.

I lock myself in a stall.

"You okay, Scarlett?" Gretchen almost manages to sound concerned.

"Come on, Gretch," Alison says.

"I think she's crying."

"No, I'm not!"

"Whatever."

I wait in the stall until I'm sure they're gone. A part of me knows that I'm acting totally irrational, as if I'm outside my own body watching a crazy person. And then a new coldness washes over me. What if Gretchen tells Mom that she saw me crying like a big baby?

The bathroom door bangs behind me as I head out into the hall. Keeping my head bowed low, I push past the people in the hallway and run out of the school.

CHAPTER 11

A Spoonful of Secrets

WHAT AM I DOING? WHERE am I even going? I hurry past stores, practically knocking down an old man pulling along a battered shopping cart. I almost get hit as a truck grinds to a stop in the middle of the crosswalk. All the time I'm heading toward home—but I don't want to go home. Future blog posts flash into my head: "Help! My Selfish Daughter Tried to Run Away," or worse, "Help! My Daughter Ran Away and Then, Unfortunately, Came Back!"

Panting for breath, I finally stop. I'm standing on the doorstep of Mrs. Simpson's house. I get the key out from under the mat, open the door, and let myself in.

The cat is there just inside the door. I scoop it up and sob into its black fur. It purrs in my arms but flicks its tail, like it's deciding whether or not to tolerate me.

"I'm sorry," I say, setting it down. "You've got your own problems, haven't you?"

The cat struts into the kitchen, meowing for food. I follow slowly behind, my heart finally easing in the calm quiet of Mrs. Simpson's kitchen. The recipe notebook is on the book stand where I left it. But I'm almost positive I left it open on the scones page. Now, it's flipped open to a page on Pat-a-Cake Oatmeal Bars. There's a drawing cut from an old book and pasted on the page of a little boy in a puffy white baker's hat. Around him, there's a hand-drawn border of steaming pies and frosted cakes.

I flip through the notebook, my mouth watering at the possibilities: Hansel and Gretel's Gingerbread, Knave of Hearts Strawberry Tarts, The Princess and the Pea Soup, Simple Simon's Potpie. But in the end, I turn back to the Pat-a-Cake Oatmeal Bars. Whatever they are, I need to make them.

Just like before, nearly every ingredient called for in the recipe is on hand as though some kind of magic baking elf has been at work. Next to the recipe book, there are even two bars of Belgian cooking chocolate on the counter that I swear weren't there last time. It's definitely a little weird, but I decide to make the best of it. I put on an apron, wash my hands, and get started. I even remember to preheat the oven this time.

The cat sits and watches as I work. First, I read through the recipe so I know exactly what I'm doing. Then, I measure out the "wet" ingredients—butter, corn syrup, a dollop of honey—into a pan. I add the brown sugar and cinnamon, and place the pan on top of the stove. I swirl the ingredients around with a wooden spoon over a low heat. The colors mix together—warm shades of brown and gold, marbled through with the bright yellow of the butter. The spicy scent goes straight to my head. It's fun watching all the separate parts of the mixture melt together like they've always belonged that way. When everything is uniform and liquid, I take the sticky mixture off the stove and stir in the instant oats. The ingredients clump on the spoon. I scrape some off with my finger and taste it. It melts on my tongue, wholesome and delicious.

I'm so caught up in what I'm doing that when the doorbell rings, I practically jump out of my apron.

I'm not expecting to get lucky a second time. I'm sure it's Mr. Kruffs, or maybe even the police. My heart starts to thump, but to be honest, what I'm the most worried about is the syrup mixture getting cold before I can finish stirring in the oats.

I open the door. Standing there is the one person I didn't expect to see after the way I acted at school: Violet.

And I'm very glad to see her.

"Can I come in?" she says.

"Sure." I stand aside and she comes inside the house. She sets down her backpack, and next to it, the empty Easter basket.

"Everyone loved the scones," she says. "That cinnamon— it really packed a punch. And it was even better because no one could figure out who made them."

"That's good." I nod uneasily. It's just so weird that the whole school was talking about the scones I made, which is the last thing I wanted. I turn and she follows me to the kitchen.

I go back to the pan and keep stirring the oats into the sticky mixture.

"What are you making?" Violet looks over my shoulder.

"Oatmeal bars." I wave a sticky hand at the recipe book. "With Belgian chocolate on top."

"Yum," Violet says. She reaches behind the book stand and picks up a can that I hadn't noticed was there. "Look," she says, reading the label. "Caramel. I love caramel." She hesitates. "Maybe you could add some of that too."

"Maybe," I say. "Can you grab me that pan?"

"Sure." She hands me a rectangular cake pan that I've

already lined with baking paper. I scoop in the clumpy mixture and pat it down with the wooden spoon. When it's all spread out and flat, I carry the pan over to the oven.

"How long does it need to cook for?"

I glance over at the book. "Twenty-five minutes." She opens the oven door and sets the timer. I put the pan inside.

"Would you like some hot chocolate?" Violet asks. "I *can* boil some water."

"Yeah, hot chocolate sounds good." I wash my hands at the sink.

Violet fills a kettle and switches it on. I find the cupboard with the mugs. Mrs. Simpson's mugs are pretty, all different colors of stoneware, some with stripes and polka dots. I give Violet a purple mug and use a blue one for me. She finishes making the hot chocolate and brings it over to the table. We sit facing each other.

"Look, I'm sorry about earlier," I say. "It's just…well…" The words stick to the roof of my mouth. "Lots of things."

"No worries," she says. "I'm the one who should be sorry."

Something unspoken seems to pass between us—one of those weird moments where you just know what the other person's thinking, and you don't have to bother with talking. But then it's gone, as Violet asks the question I've been expecting.

"So, your mom's really that blogger?"

"Yeah." *That* blogger. Enough said.

"I hadn't heard of the blog, but Gretchen showed me. She said you guys used to be friends, but then when your mom got famous, you started acting all stuck-up."

"Stuck-up?" I stare at her dumbfounded. "Me?"

"I said you didn't seem like that to me. And I read some of the blog."

"You did?" I lean forward, feeling tense.

"I know your mom doesn't mention your name. But everyone at school seems to know about it. I couldn't believe she wrote all that personal stuff about you. You know…the stuff about you washing your white underwear with black socks, giving your whole family head lice, and wetting the bed till you were eight." Her face is solemn. "I know how I would feel…"

"How?"

"Embarrassed," she says immediately. "And also kind of sad."

I smile weakly. And then I find myself telling Violet just how embarrassing and "kind of sad" it is for me for real. I tell her about Stacie, and about how Gretchen and Alison pretended to be my friends, but really they were leaking stuff to Mom. I tell her about the violin, the tap-dancing, and the

Mom Survival Kit. Then, I tell her about Dad leaving, and about Mom's online "victory" over him. I tell her how Mom's most popular post is the one about "Top Ten Reasons I Wish I'd Never Had Kids," and where does that leave me? And when I've finished telling her all that, a tear falls into the lukewarm hot chocolate in the mug in front of me.

She puts a hand on my arm. "I didn't tell anyone you made the scones, Scarlett. Honest." She hesitates. "I wanted to, though. Because you should get the credit."

"I know I'm being totally paranoid. But it's just that I don't want anything—*anything*—to get back to Mom. I can't stand her writing about me. I—" A sob escapes. "I just hate it. Every week when her blog post goes up, I want to crawl into a hole and die."

"Have you told her?"

"Told her?" As soon as the words are out, I realize that, despite trying to be friendly, Violet will never understand. "Yeah, I did try. I told her it made everyone laugh at me. I told her I have no friends anymore, and that I don't want to do anything if she's going to write about it."

"So what happened?"

"We had a 'discussion' about it. She told me her side— that she's working really hard to be successful with the blog, and get advertisers and stuff. She said she wanted to have a job where she could support me and my sister without working long hours away from home. She tried to tell me all about online demographics and unique visitors—most of it, I didn't really understand. I told her I supported her goals, but the things she said really hurt sometimes. So, I thought we'd come to an understanding. I felt good for a few days. Until the next post came out. Guess what it was about?"

"Your talk?"

"Bingo." I sigh. "It was called 'The Ungrateful Teenage Muse' or something like that. You can guess what it said."

"Yeah."

"The only thing that kind of works is doing nothing— and I mean nothing at all. No clubs, no activities, no friends, nothing. She can't get as much mileage out of boring as she can out of failure."

"Must be pretty lonely."

"I guess so." I shrug.

Her heart-shaped face brightens as she smiles. "It's good then that you're doing something about it."

"Doing? What am I doing?"

"You're cooking." She sniffs the air as the smell of baking oatmeal bars gets stronger and stronger.

I lean forward with a stab of real fear. "Violet, please. I'm not really going to *do* anything. I can't—I mean, I'm breaking into my neighbor's house and using all her stuff. If Mom found out and wrote about it, I'd probably be arrested or something."

"Well, I won't tell…on one condition." Her smile grows mischievous.

"What's that?"

"I want to cook with you. We can teach ourselves—just us. It will be a secret."

"But—" I open my mouth to protest. There are a thousand things wrong with the idea. Instead, just for a second, I let myself be swept along by Violet's enthusiasm. "A cooking club?" I glance around me at the amazing kitchen, mulling over the idea.

"Yeah. A *secret* cooking club."

"Hmm." I stand as the oven beeps that it's done. "Can I think about it?"

CHAPTER 12

A Dash of Friendship

THE OATMEAL BARS TURN HONEY brown in the oven. I take them out quickly so they don't get burnt. They smell rich, buttery, and delicious. I put the pan on a wire rack to cool. For the next step, Violet opens the can of caramel and scoops it into a bowl while I melt the chocolate over a pan of hot water.

"I never really thought about trying to cook or bake anything before," Violet says. She looks at a penciled-in note in the margin of the recipe and then mixes some salt into the caramel. "I mean, my mom used to cook everything, and I guess I always thought there'd be time to learn—"

She stops. I pause in my stirring and look sideways at her. She bites her lip for a second, and then her mouth upturns in its usual amused expression. But her eyes don't look amused.

She stares at the caramel, swirling the wooden spoon through it absently. I want to ask her what's up, but just then I notice the chocolate has completely melted, so I take it off the stove.

"Quick," I say, "let's get this on before it starts to harden. You go first." We both take our bowls over to the table where I've put the oatmeal bars to cool. Violet spoons an even layer of caramel over the top. I keep stirring the chocolate, and when she's done the whole pan, I spoon a thick layer on top. When I've finished, Violet uses the handle of the spoon to write something in the cooling chocolate:

The Secret Cooking Club

She hands me the spoon. I underline the words with a squiggle. It all seems very solemn and official. But then my stomach breaks the mood by growling loudly. "It looks good," I say. "I can't wait to taste it."

After we've cleaned up the mess and the chocolate has set a little, I cut it into squares and serve up two pieces on Mrs. Simpson's rose-patterned china. Violet and I clink our mugs together. Then we each take a bite.

"Gosh." Violet grins. "It's good."

"It *is* good." I can hear the pride in my own voice. It's

crunchy and gooey, and I can taste both the chocolate and the caramel. It all melts together in my mouth. I've had oatmeal bars lots of times—the kind wrapped in plastic from the corner store. But this is completely different. This is homemade. And *I* made it. *We.* I take another bite, chewing it slowly. Part of me almost wants to tell Mom. *Almost.*

I lick a streak of chocolate off my lips. "What are we going to do with them?" I say. "We can't eat them all."

"I could give it a try," Violet jokes. Then her smile wavers. "But I guess it's up to you."

"No. It's up to *us*." I savor the word. "We're a club now."

Violet takes a bite, chewing thoughtfully. "I know you've got issues about it. But I really liked giving out the free samples at school. It was weird, but it made everybody a little bit nicer somehow."

"Nicer?"

"Yeah. I think so. And if we did it again, we can say they were made by the Secret Cooking Club." Violet wipes her chin. "It'll seem as if there are lots of us doing it."

"You mean, like we're some kind of underground network who are all taking turns making things?"

Violet's eyes shine. "It would be cool, wouldn't it? Especially if what we make actually tastes good. And just

about anything is bound to taste better than cafeteria food."
She sticks out her tongue. "That rice pudding they serve every
other day tastes like puke."

"It looks like it as well." I giggle. "All those lumps."

"Gross!" She laughs too. "So, you're in?"

"Well…" I have to admit, the idea does sound cool. And if
a little sugar rush makes school a happier place, then who am
I to complain?

"Unless you have a better idea?"

"I don't," I say. "Though I did think maybe we could
bake something for Mrs. Simpson. If she's still in the hospital,
she must be hating the food too. We could bring her a pan of
oatmeal bars."

"That's a great idea." Violet says. "Let's do it."

"But I like your idea about school too," I say. "As long you
solemnly swear on your life that no one will know I'm involved."

"Okay," Violet says. "I swear." We shake sticky hands
to seal the deal. Then we eat another square each and drink
another mug of hot chocolate.

"Um, Violet," I say, licking the crumbs from my lips. "I
think we might need another batch."

CHAPTER 13

A Nameless Gift

VIOLET AND I MAKE TWO more batches of oatmeal bars, talking about all the things we could make next. The possibilities are endless, and it's nice to have someone who's as excited as I am. As I'm spreading the final layer of chocolate over the salted caramel, Violet comes to the table with a little jar. "I found these," she says. "Crystallized Violets. It says on the jar they're real flowers."

The jar is filled with sparkly purple flower petals coated with glittered sugar. I open it and hold it up to my nose. They smell very sweet.

"Do you want to put them on top?" I say.

"Well, I don't know. It might make for kind of funny oatmeal bars. But it could throw people off the scent that you had anything to do with it."

"Okay. Let's do it."

Violet arranges the crystallized violets in a swirl pattern. The purple sparkles look like magic dust. I don't know how it's going to taste, but Violet seems to have a flair for making things look pretty.

We put the oatmeal bars for Mrs. Simpson into Violet's Easter basket. For the school ones, we fill up a big container with a picture of Peter Rabbit on it that we found in a cupboard. I wrap up the last two oatmeal bars for Violet and me to take home. I leave the little notebook of recipes on the book stand—it seems to have done a pretty good job keeping our secret so far, and it belongs in Rosemary's Kitchen.

We're in the middle of cleaning up when there's a muffled ringing sound. Violet's phone. She checks the screen and gasps. "It's seven o'clock already. I have to go."

"Seven?" I can't believe it's that late. I was planning to tell Mom that I'd gone to the library again, but it closes at five. The words flash in my head: "My Daughter Went Missing for Two Hours: Was She Smoking, Kissing, Drinking, or Shoplifting?"

I'll have to think of something else.

I quickly finish the washing up while Violet wipes the counter. Whatever spell we've been under is broken. Now, all the problems with our plan seep into my head. What if the hospital won't let us in? What if Mrs. Simpson is in a coma...or what if she passed away? What if someone at school sees me or Violet putting out the oatmeal bars? What if the crystallized violets taste disgusting? *What if? What if...?*

"I'm not sure about this," I say. My chest feels as if it's being squeezed by a giant fist.

"It will be okay," Violet says. "I promise. Let's just give it a shot."

I force myself to take a breath. "Okay."

CHAPTER 14

The Big Laugh-In

WHEN I GET HOME, THERE'S no sign that Mom's even noticed I was gone. Kelsie's sitting in front of the TV watching *The Ice Princess*, her eyes glued to the screen. Her mouth is crusted with dried chocolate from a half-eaten package of Pepperidge Farm cookies. The door to the Mom Cave is shut. I unwrap the oatmeal bar, cut it into two pieces, and set it on a plate in the kitchen. I don't have my backpack or my homework, so I sit on the sofa next to my sister and eat a bag of potato chips.

As I'm trying to tune out my sister's off-key rendition of the theme song, Mom bursts into the room.

"Oatmeal bars!" she cries. "I've been absolutely craving oatmeal bars all day. I mean, I didn't know it was oatmeal bars

I wanted exactly…" She brushes a strand of unwashed hair off her face. "But where on earth did they come from?"

"From me," I say. "Some kids at school made them. They were giving out free samples."

"I love the purple sparkly things," Mom says, chomping happily on her piece of oatmeal bar. "And the caramel. It reminds me of something else my grandma—" Frowning, she cuts herself off. "You should do something like that, Scarlett." She looks at the empty bag of chips in my lap. The cogs in her brain are clearly ticking. "Help! There's a New Cooking Club at School and My Lazy, Deadbeat Daughter Won't Get Off Her Rear End and Stop Eating Chips."

"Yeah, Mom," I say with a shrug. "I probably should."

At school the next day, I sit at the back of math class, watching Gretchen and Alison text each other under the table. Just before lunchtime, Violet raises her hand and asks to go to the bathroom. She gives me a quick glance on her way out. I feel a little thrill of fear and anticipation.

In the cafeteria, I sit at a corner table and watch the kids coming in—some with their lunch bags, others taking a tray and getting a hot lunch (some kind of chicken goopy stuff with clumpy pudding for dessert). While on her "bathroom break," Violet has placed the container with the oatmeal bars on the center table with a little sign that says FREE SAMPLES FROM THE SECRET COOKING CLUB. Violet herself comes into the cafeteria a few minutes later, flanked by a laughing Gretchen and Alison. I deliberately look away from them.

Someone approaches the basket—none other than Nick Farr. His brown eyes widen. He looks around quickly and takes a piece. And then he's looking in my direction and smiling.

OMG. Nick Farr is looking at me. He's walking toward me. Somehow he knows—he must. He...

...walks past me and sits at a nearby table with a group of his friends. I exhale sharply. What was I thinking?

"Check this out," he says to his friends, pointing at the center table. "The Secret Cooking Club."

"Killer," one of them replies. He and another friend stand and walk to the center table. They each grab a little piece of oatmeal bar and eat it, and then another. Another of Nick's friends comes up and pretends he's going to grab the whole container and stick it under his shirt. More people come up in a steady stream: two girls who are part of the goth crowd, three star soccer players, two girls on the swim team, a couple of computer geeks, and then, horning their way to the front of the line, Gretchen and Alison.

Gretchen wrinkles her pert little upturned nose as she looks inside the container. Her voice is high-pitched enough that I can hear her over the din. "What are those things on top?" she says to Alison.

"I don't know. But if I eat any of them, my face will break out!"

The girls make a point of flouncing off without trying any oatmeal bars. Their rejection ruins the mood. Except for the computer geeks who come back for seconds, the crowd begins to dwindle.

Suddenly, from one of the far tables across the room, there's a loud snort of laughter. A few people turn to look. It's a tall girl with a neon-pink streak in her black hair. She's one of the goth crowd too. They aren't the kind of kids who ever smile, but that's exactly what they're doing. The girl whispers to her friend and hands her a tiny piece of oatmeal bar.

"OMG, it's fab," the friend says. Before I know it, everyone's talking and laughing, and people are splitting their oatmeal bars apart to make sure everyone can try them. The good feeling seems to move like a chain reaction from one to the other. From person to person, table to table. The sugar rush seems to be making everyone happy.

Gretchen looks at Alison. I can tell they're on the verge of trying to ruin everything, but then Nick comes up and whispers something in Gretchen's ear. Gretchen gives him a flirty smile and goes back to the center table and takes an oatmeal bar. I watch as the transformation comes over her—she goes back to Nick and whispers something in his ear, and they both start laughing their heads off. It's so loud that two teachers come over. They glance around, looking surprised, and then they smile too. The basket of oatmeal bars empties quickly, but the positive vibe is still there in the room. I'm even more shocked to realize I'm smiling at the whole ridiculous thing. I spot Violet standing near the door. She's not laughing, but her bow-shaped lips are turned up in satisfaction. I walk toward her, but the bell rings, and by the time I get over to the door, she's gone.

CHAPTER 15

Mrs. Simpson

THE OATMEAL BARS ARE LONG gone, but that afternoon, there's still a lively buzz in the classroom—more people than usual speaking up and asking questions in class, talking to people they wouldn't normally talk to, and generally more smiles all around. When it's time to go home, I meet up with Violet in the hallway. Together we push through the crowds to the front entrance, and out to the parking lot.

"Everyone *loved* the oatmeal bars," she says. "Just like we hoped."

"I know. I didn't expect people to like them quite so much." I shiver a little knowing that *Nick* liked them.

"Maybe it was the crystallized violets," she says with a grin.

"Well, they definitely made a change from that gross pudding!"

"That's for sure," Violet says. "Anyway, we'd better get going."

"Going? Where are we going?"

"To see Mrs. Simpson, remember? Do you know which hospital she's in?" Violet's question throws me.

"Um, no."

"Well, Riverside Medical is closest, so let's try there first. There's a bus, I think."

"Okay." I shrug, knowing Violet's right. Oatmeal bars or not, visiting Mrs. Simpson is the right thing to do. "Let's go."

The bus stop is around the corner from school, and we don't have to wait long. Twenty minutes later, the bus drops us off in front of the hospital. It's a busy, intimidating place, with cars and vans coming and going, old people and pregnant women meandering over the crosswalk, people in wheelchairs, and nurses in uniforms going in and out.

Violet leads the way inside. There's a gift shop and a coffee kiosk in the lobby, and at one side, a reception desk. Violet goes up to the receptionist and speaks confidently, like she's been in a hospital lots of times and isn't even a little bit scared.

"We're here to visit a patient," she says. "Mrs. Simpson."

The woman looks over her half-moon glasses at Violet and me. "Which ward is she in?"

"I'm not sure." Violet looks at me.

"Her name is Rosemary Simpson," I say, trying to sound like a grown-up. "Can you direct us to the right ward?"

The woman types something into the computer one finger at a time. It seems to take forever. Finally, she looks up again. "Are you relations?"

"Yes," I say without hesitation. "I'm her niece. She's my only aunt, and I'm really worried about her. My friend and I brought her a basket of treats we made."

The woman frowns. "She's in the Hessel Wing. Follow the blue line to B ward."

We follow the painted blue line on the floor through bleak hallways, past outpatients hurrying to appointments in worrying-sounding departments such as oncology, radiotherapy, physical rehabilitation, and prenatal care. With our basket and backpacks, Violet and I are like two Little Red Riding Hoods wandering through a scary forest of machines, fluorescent lights, and sick people. Finally, the blue line ends in a door marked Hessel Wing, Ward B. I push open the heavy swinging door.

Inside is another reception desk with two nurses in

pale-blue uniforms. One is shuffling through paperwork, the other is typing on a computer. I'm relieved when Violet goes up to the desk. She says who we are and who we're here to see.

"Rosemary Simpson?" The nurse with the paperwork looks at the other nurse. "Is she allowed visitors?"

"I suppose so," the other woman says, still staring at the computer screen. "But she's been given a mild sedative. She has a concussion and needs to be kept here under observation."

"Can we see her?" I say. "We brought her a basket with some oatmeal bars that we made."

"She won't be eating any oatmeal bars. But since you're relations"—the nurse eyes me skeptically—"you can have five minutes to see her. And you can leave the basket here if you like."

I get the feeling that if we leave the oatmeal bars, she and the other nurse will eat up what's inside. Violet obviously thinks the same as she clutches the basket even more tightly.

The nurse points down the hallway. "She's in room six. Be back here in five minutes."

"Five minutes," I repeat. Violet and I walk quickly down the hall. "What a horrible place," I whisper.

Violet doesn't answer. She seems lost in a world of her own. "Yeah," she says finally as we reach the door to room six. Game show music is blaring loudly from inside.

I look into the room. There are two raised beds, one on each side of the room. In the bed closest to the door is a white-haired woman who's staring at the television and eating a heart-shaped box of candies. There are lots of flowers and get-well cards on her bedside table. Clearly, she's being well looked after. In the other bed is a gray figure, little more than a lump underneath the thin, blue blanket. There's a breathing tube sticking out of her nose, an IV in her arm, and she's hooked up to a monitor that is blipping slowly in the corner. There are no flowers or get-well cards anywhere.

I walk into the room. "Shh," the white-haired woman says. "They're about to solve the puzzle."

On the television screen, a woman is turning over letters. "Too bad," the host says to the losing contestant.

"Huh, it wasn't bad luck at all—he was just dumb," the old woman says, gesturing with the heart-shaped box. Her accent sounds British or something. She glares, as if noticing Violet and me for the first time. "Who are you?"

"We're looking for Mrs. Simpson. Is that her?" I point to the blanket bulge, already knowing the answer.

"What's left of her." The old woman frowns.

"We brought this." Violet holds up the basket on her arm. "We thought she might be sick of hospital food."

The woman pops a candy in her mouth. "Nice of you, dear. But I don't think she'll be up to it any time soon."

"Has she been awake?" I ask.

The woman flips through the TV channels with the remote. "Oh aye," she says, her eyes wide. "She's been awake—off and on. And let me tell you, it's hard to get any sleep when she is." She shakes her head and *tsks*. "Tussling with the blankets and moaning about her cat. She wants to go home, but her nephew won't have it."

"Nephew?" Violet asks.

"You mean Mr. Kruffs?" I say.

"Aye, that's him. So you know him, do you?"

"No, but I've seen the election posters—"

"Election." She snorts. "Well, good luck to him, that's all I can say. Slipping in here, making her upset. I've thought about asking to be moved to another room, but in here"—she laughs grimly—"one old dear is as good as the next." She settles on a channel and turns up the volume. "At least she's asleep most of the time."

From the other bed there's a loud groan and a rustling noise. The gray old woman under the blanket coughs and splutters, then wriggles in the bed like she's trying to prop herself up on her elbows. Her eyes are open, but glassy, as though she's not really seeing anything in the room. Her head turns slightly and she spies the basket. She leans forward and sniffs the air. Her blue eyes meet mine.

"Mrs. Simpson?" I whisper as Violet and I walk toward her. "We've made you some oatmeal bars. They're chocolate and salted caramel."

The old woman sinks back into the bed. Her eyes close again, her lips drawn into a thin line. But then she seems to smile. Her breathing grows even as she goes back to sleep.

"Maybe she'll be able to try them later," I say to Violet in a low voice. Violet nods and sets the basket down on Mrs. Simpson's bedside table. I reach out and touch Mrs. Simpson's gnarled hand. "Get well soon," I say softly.

Violet and I tiptoe out of the room.

CHAPTER 16

Banoffee

VIOLET AND I DON'T SAY much as we ride the bus back. I secretly vow to avoid hospitals in the future at all costs. I keep thinking about Mrs. Simpson—a helpless bulge under a thin blanket. I know it was the right thing to visit her, but I kind of wish we hadn't. I'd rather think of Rosemary Simpson as the amazing cook with the fabulous kitchen. She did seem to revive a little when she smelled the oatmeal bars, though. I hope she gets to taste them.

Violet stares out the window of the bus. As the sky grows darker and her reflection in the window sharpens, I'm startled to see a tear trickling down her cheek. I turn away not to embarrass her. The bus stops near the school, and we both get off.

"So I guess I'll see you tomorrow?" I try hard to sound cheery.

She shrugs. The tears are gone, but there are dark hollows under her eyes. "Okay."

I wait for her to turn around or walk off—I don't even know where she lives—but she keeps on walking along beside me.

I turn down my street. We walk together, passing several houses with EMORY KRUFFS FOR CITY COUNCIL signs in their windows. We reach the last two houses at the end of the street: my house and Mrs. Simpson's.

"I'm going to feed the cat," I announce.

Violet looks at me. She smiles.

I unlock Mrs. Simpson's door, and we go inside. Right away, I can tell something's wrong.

"Where's the cat?" I whisper. My skin prickles with goose bumps.

"Maybe it's asleep?"

"But it's always been waiting here before."

Inside, there's no sign of the cat, and other things are different too. Mrs. Simpson's pictures have been taken off the wall and stacked against each other, and a lot of her knick-knacks have been cleared away. There are a few open boxes with bubble wrap spilling out. Mrs. Simpson is obviously in no condition for spring cleaning, so it can only be one person—Mr. Kruffs. The idea that he's been here gives me the creeps.

Violet seems to have the same thought. "What if he's still here?" she says anxiously.

We stand still, listening for sounds from upstairs or inside the kitchen. Everything is quiet.

I straighten my shoulders. "We're not doing anything wrong. We're only here to feed the cat."

"Maybe we should leave."

"I'm staying," I say. "We may never get another chance to be here. You can go if you want to." I give her a sideways glance. "But I'd rather you didn't."

Her violet eyes widen with shared understanding. "Okay," she says. "What should we make tonight?"

The kitchen has avoided being ransacked, but only barely. The cat's bed and food dish are gone—at least whoever took the cat away is going to feed it. There are other things different too: dirty cups in the sink, a list of moving companies on the counter, and the little book of recipes is off its wooden book stand. I notice how tattered its binding is, how faded the cover. It's covered with crumbs, like someone used it for a cutting board to make a sandwich on.

I pick up the book and blow off the crumbs. I set it back on the book stand and open it up at random. It falls open almost automatically to a recipe for Georgie Porgie's Banoffee Pie.

"Banoffee Pie!" Violet says. "That's my favorite dessert in the whole world."

I lower my eyes. "I don't think I've ever had it." I skim over the ingredients. Banana and toffee—not two things I would ever have thought of putting together—plus lots of cream.

"Are you serious? Then we have to make it!"

Violet's excitement wins me over—that, and the fact that there's a fruit bowl in the center of the table that has a big bunch of fresh bananas in it. Some things are just meant to be, I guess.

"Okay," I say, "let's do it."

The rest of the ingredients aren't on hand this time. It's as if the magic kitchen elves have all fled after Mr. Kruffs's visit. We have to dig through the cupboards to find a packet of graham crackers, a can of condensed milk, and a half-used pack of brown sugar. In the very back of the fridge, we find the cream and butter.

When everything is assembled, I read through the recipe again. "Look at him," Violet says over my shoulder, pointing to the cartoon-like picture of fat little Georgie Porgie. He's chasing a flock of merry girls with his lips pursed in a kiss.

"He's gross." She makes a face. "I wouldn't want him to kiss me. Unless he happened to grow up to be a boy like Nick Farr."

My insides shake. "Nick Farr?"

"He's cute, isn't he?" She laughs.

"Yeah." There seems to be no point in lying.

I turn on the stove, ready to melt the butter. For some reason, I feel kind of nervous and on edge—it could be the hospital visit, or the intruder that was here. But if I'm being honest, it's probably Violet's mention of Nick Farr.

Violet squishes the graham crackers into crumbs and tips them into the pan. As I stir them into the butter, I begin to feel a little calmer.

"Do you think he'll come back?" Violet says.

"Who?" I say, startled.

"Mr. Kruffs. It's kind of creepy that he's been here."

I look around Rosemary's Kitchen. It seems lonely without the cat. "Maybe Mr. Kruffs has permission to be here, I don't know…" I trail off. "I wish there was something we could do to help Mrs. Simpson."

Violet brings over some pans from the cupboard. We press the crumbly mixture in the bottom and then put the whole thing in the fridge to set. "Like what?" she says.

I shake my head. "Right now, I don't have a clue."

CHAPTER 17

Secret Samples

I REALLY DON'T KNOW WHAT to do about Mrs. Simpson. But I do know that making the banoffee pie is a blast. Violet and I triple the recipe—so we have enough for us, plus lots of free samples for school. Luckily, Rosemary's Kitchen has plenty of bowls and pie pans.

Making the filling is sweet and sticky and messy and fun. We gorge ourselves on bananas and licking out the bowls. Then we talk and laugh and look through the cupboards while the pies set in the fridge. I find several large chocolate bars and take them out.

"The recipe says to decorate the pies with chocolate curls," I say, pointing to the book.

"We can use these too." Violet takes out a container of

baking decorations—sprinkles of all sizes and colors, icing bags and colors, even gold leaf you can eat.

When the pies have chilled, we take them out one by one—two round ones, and two that we made in containers shaped like a heart and a gingerbread man. "Look, it's Georgie Porgie," I say when I take the swirly banana cream man out of the fridge. We both laugh.

I make the chocolate curls using a vegetable peeler like the recipe book says to do. Violet decorates Georgie Porgie with little icing stars and a tie made of multicolored sprinkles. She gives him eyes of chocolate buttons and an icing nose and mouth. I can't help laughing as I add his hair of chocolate curls—I've never seen such a fancy pie before, and Georgie Porgie looks nothing like Nick Farr. Violet laughs too and gives him a collar and belt of crystallized violets. He ends up looking like a large, goopy snowman.

On the heart-shaped pie, Violet writes "The Secret Cooking Club" in big, loopy icing letters, and I cover the rest in sprinkles and chocolate curls. Finally, we're done.

"They look fab," I say, beaming. We find some deep Tupperware cake containers to use to take the pies to school tomorrow. Then we sit and eat the little round one we've made for ourselves.

The pie is gooey and moist, and the taste of toffee and fresh banana seems like the most natural combination of flavors in the whole world.

"Mmm," Violet purrs, taking a bite. "This is the best."

I let cool sweet cream settle on my tongue for a second before swallowing. It's delicious and sweet, but not too sweet—like Goldilocks's porridge, it's just right. I still can't believe we've made it ourselves. But we did!

"We'll need plastic bowls and spoons for school." I lick the cream off my upper lip. "It's pretty gooey."

"Yeah," Violet says between bites. "We can get them at the store on the way to school. Do you have any money?"

"I've got some saved from my allowance. I can use that."

We clean everything up and put the pies back in Mrs. Simpson's fridge to chill overnight. We agree that I'll come and get them tomorrow before school.

It's dark by the time we leave the house, and stepping outside is like plunging into a cold bath. Nothing seems real to me anymore, other than Rosemary's Kitchen. Violet seems unusually quiet, as if she feels the same as me.

"You okay?" I ask. We stand at the dim edge of a circle of streetlight.

"Yeah." Violet nods. "See you tomorrow." She turns and

starts walking. I stand there watching her go until she turns the corner and disappears.

This time when I get home, I'm not so lucky as before. Mom is in the kitchen, frantically calling people on her phone, looking for me.

"Seriously, Scarlett," she says, "I was worried sick. Where have you been?"

I sit at the table, feeling exhausted. I wish I could tell Mom everything—about the hospital, the cooking, Mrs. Simpson, and how we have to save her from Mr. Kruffs. And about the excellent banoffee pie we made. I open my mouth and close it again. I can't tell Mom anything. If I do, I'll only regret it.

"Sorry, Mom," I say, half meaning it. "There's a new girl at school—I went over to her house. We're working on a project together for science."

Mom doesn't ask the girl's name, and I don't volunteer it. She shakes her head. "Honestly, Scarlett. I mean, I know you don't want to talk to me anymore, but you really can't do that kind of thing."

"I'm sorry, Mom. It's just that…" I take a breath. I'm

going to tell her how I feel. I'm going to see if we can be friends again. I'm going to—

"Don't do it again." Her face is red as she checks her watch. "I'm so behind. My guest post for the Scary Kids website is due tomorrow. I can't believe how thoughtless you are sometimes."

She turns and marches off into the Mom Cave. The door slams behind her. With a big sigh, I go upstairs to my room and crawl into bed. I dream of a flock of girls chasing a pie-shaped Nick Farr, whose eyes meet mine as he runs away.

The next morning I wake up with butterflies in my stomach. I find my allowance box in my sock drawer and open it. There are a few loose coins in the bottom, but the ten-dollar bill I had inside is gone. I groan softly. Not only does Mom often forget to give me my allowance, but she's always "borrowing" money from me when she forgets to go to the ATM.

Snores are coming from Mom's room, and I don't want to wake her. Instead, I head downstairs to the Mom Cave where she keeps her purse. As usual, her desk is a mess. There are papers everywhere—crumpled drafts of articles and blog posts, letters from Superdrug and glossy photos of the Survival

Kit packaging. I'm struck by how hard Mom is working to keep her blog empire going.

I find Mom's purse and "re-borrow" my money, scribbling on a yellow sticky note to let her know. Underneath the bag there's a piece of paper—a printout of something she's writing, half of which is crossed out in red pen. My stomach knots as I skim over the uncrossed-out part.

"Me Against Her: Why Have We Grown So Apart?"

It starts out in a joking way, stuff like: "I never wanted to be one of those pushy parents. But now I see I messed up big-time. I mean, if I'd known my daughter was going to hate me by the time she was a teenager, I should have made sure she was a concert pianist."

I read on. Instead of going into the usual stuff, I'm surprised by what she's written. "Lately, something weird has happened. I've started remembering what it was like to be *her* age. It began when I had a craving for macaroni and cheese— the way my grandma used to make it. And I started wondering: How does *she* feel, and have I really been paying attention...?"

The paragraph is scribbled out in red pen. But the words are there in black and white.

· CHAPTER 18 ·

In the Hall

VIOLET IS WAITING FOR ME in front of the store. I've got the three Tupperware containers in a huge burlap bag I found in Rosemary's Kitchen. We've got just enough money to buy a package of plastic bowls and spoons and some baking powder, which we're almost out of at Mrs. Simpson's.

"It's your turn today," she says as we're on our way out.

"My turn? For what?"

"To set up the secret samples. You just have to make sure you get to the cafeteria before everyone else. And don't forget to make a sign to put on the table."

"Me?" My heart thumps in alarm. "I thought you were going to do it."

"I did it last time. I mean, I can't go to the bathroom every day at the same time, can I?"

"I don't know." We walk on in silence as worry fizzes in my veins. What if someone notices me sneaking three creamy mountains of banoffee pie into the cafeteria? Word travels fast around school. It isn't just me I'm worried about, but the Secret Cooking Club. It may only be Violet and me, but if I lose that, then what's left?

The morning flies by. I try to focus on misplaced commas and then algebra, but I keep staring at the clock as it gets nearer and nearer to the time when I'm supposed to raise my hand and ask if I can go to the bathroom. Twenty minutes to go, then ten, then five.

Just as I'm about to raise my hand, Nick Farr beats me to it.

"Sorry, Mrs. Fry, but I need the bathroom," he says.

The math teacher gets a boys' bathroom pass down from the wall and hands it to him.

"Uh, me too," I say in a small voice. I can feel the redness creeping over my face as someone behind me snickers.

The teacher puts her hands on her hips. "Lunch is in fifteen minutes. Can't you wait?"

"No, Mrs. Fry." My skin crawls with the eyes of everyone

looking at me. When the banoffee pie turns up in the cafeteria, everyone will certainly know it was me.

But what can I do? I look pleadingly in Violet's direction, but she's staring at her notebook, her blue-black hair a curtain in front of her face. With an irritated sigh, the teacher gives me a girls' bathroom pass. I hold my breath until I'm across the room and out the door.

The hallway is empty—no sign of Nick. I hurry down the hall to the vacant Food and Nutrition classroom where I've stowed the burlap bag of banoffee pies in the refrigerator. They're right where I left them, along with the bag of plastic bowls and spoons. I scoop everything up and go back into the hallway. I rush past the bathrooms toward the cafeteria. If anyone spots me now—

A door swooshes open just behind me.

I'm caught!

I can feel eyes on my back. *His* eyes. Nick Farr. Captain of the soccer team, star science student, good friend of Gretchen, Alison, and all the popular girls. Admired by the rest of us from afar—but in this case, not far enough.

"Scarlett?"

His voice.

"You okay?"

I turn around, my eyes wide like a deer in the headlights.

"Yeah, fine." I force a smile.

He stares at the big bag in my hand.

"What have you got there?"

"Um, nothing." Before he can say another word, I go into the girls' bathroom. I stand there, panting, staring at my reflection in the mirror. My hair is as frazzled as I feel, and the skin of my neck is covered with guilty-looking red blotches. My mind is a whirlwind of indecision. Do I go back to the empty classroom and hide the goods? Do I continue with my mission like nothing's happened? Do I tell Violet? Try to talk to Nick and see if he'll keep it a secret? Or maybe he won't put two and two together. Okay, that's pretty unlikely.

I smooth my hair and scowl at my reflection. "Get a grip," I say to the girl staring back.

The hallway is empty when I leave the bathroom. I rush to the cafeteria; my hand is shaking as I take out the pies and set them in a row on the table. The lunch workers are talking loudly behind their little window as they do the final preparations for lunch, but they don't notice me. I get the bowls and spoons out of the bag—why didn't I take them out of the packaging before I got here?—and manage to wrestle them out of the plastic wrapping, ripping a fingernail in the process.

Finally, I unfold my sign and tape it to the edge of the table: FREE SAMPLES—FROM THE SECRET COOKING CLUB.

I turn and rush out of the cafeteria and down the hallway. I slip back into the classroom as everyone is putting away their notebooks before lunch. When I reach my seat, I can't help looking to the front of the room—where Nick Farr sits. He turns around and his gaze meets mine, just like in my dream. My stomach turns over. He gives me a wide, melting grin… then puts a finger to his lips.

CHAPTER 19

The Secret Cooking Club Strikes Again

THERE'S A RUSH OF FLUTTERING papers and scraping chairs as the class breaks for lunch. Violet gives me a knowing look from across the room and then goes to join Gretchen and Alison. I feel a stab of jealousy, but part of our cover is that Violet and I won't hang out together at school. I follow the crowds of kids to the cafeteria.

I sit at my usual table near the door. A number of people are already lined up at the center table, waiting to take a bowl of banoffee pie. It's the same as before—the goths, the sports crowd, the geeks. My heart lurches as Gretchen pushes her way to the front, flanked by Alison and Violet.

But if anyone was expecting another laugh-in, they're in for a surprise. One of the goth girls—tall and skinny with dark black eyeliner—elbows Gretchen out of the way. "There's a line, you know," she says tersely.

I hold my breath as Gretchen turns to face the girl, craning her neck. "What did you say?" she challenges.

The tall girl snorts. Two of her pale-faced friends come up on either side of her like twin phantoms. "Wait your turn."

"Get over yourself," Gretchen says. Her face has a strange grayish tinge to it… Is she sick?

The tall girl glances at her two friends, glares at Gretchen, and gives a little snort. "You know what?" she says, flicking her hand. "You go ahead. Be my guest."

Gretchen gives her a fake little PTA princess smile. She takes a big goopy piece of pie. Everyone is watching as she holds the plastic spoon to her nose, sniffs it, then takes a bite.

"Hah," the tall girl says. "You're going to get so *fat*."

The last word seems to echo around the room. For what seems like an eternity, no one speaks, or even breathes.

If there's a word in the English language for the color of Gretchen's face, then I'm sure I don't know it. At first, it turns kind of pink and spotty like she's been scratching a rash or something, but then it immediately turns a shade of greenish gray like pea soup left in the fridge too long. The spoon in her hand drops to the floor. Everybody turns to stare as her cheeks get all full and puffy, and her eyes bulge out from her face. "Watch out," Violet cries. But before anyone can even react, Gretchen's mouth opens and a volcano of vomit erupts, flying across the table and landing in a slick, brown mess all over the floor.

There's a collective gasp of horror. And then the tall goth girl shrieks, "Oh, gross—it's Retchin' Gretchen!"

"Retchin' Gretchen." The words move through the cafeteria like a river. There's the odd groan and trickles of laughter, and a growing sense of mayhem. Out of the corner of my eye, I see Violet sneak out of the room. I get up and run after her.

Outside the cafeteria, I slump against the wall. "What have we done?" I sigh at the same time she blurts out, "Our lovely pie!"

"That was so awful," I say, not sure whether I feel like laughing or crying. "We never should have given out free samples. I mean…do you think Gretchen's okay?"

Violet shrugs. "I think so. And it wasn't our pie that made her sick—she had a stomachache earlier." Her eyes grow wide. "Retchin' Gretchen." Laughter sputters from her mouth.

The cafeteria begins to empty in a mass exodus.

"I'll see you after school, okay?" Violet says.

"I don't know…" I begin walking down the hallway so

no one will see us talking. Now that our pie has humiliated Gretchen, she'll want to know who's responsible. How could I ever have allowed myself to get into this situation?

"Come on, Scarlett!" Violet says.

"Look," I say, "I can't do this anymore. If my mom finds out—"

"So that's it then?" Violet interrupts. "You're just going to let her win? Like you've been doing all along?"

I whirl around to face her, my anger boiling. "You just don't get it, do you? And luckily for you, you never will."

CHAPTER 20

The Betrayal

THE ONLY THING WORSE THAN not having anything good in my life is having something and then losing it. Thanks to Gretchen and my fight with Violet, the Secret Cooking Club dies a quick but painful death.

After school, instead of going to Mrs. Simpson's house, I go to the library. I've always been good at school stuff, so I'm able to finish my homework quickly. I read through a couple of science magazines, trying to get interested in something. But all I can think about is how much I miss Violet, and which recipes we might have tried if things had been different. I even forget to worry too much about Mom's upcoming blog post. Even if she's somehow heard about Gretchen, there's nothing to link me to what happened.

Gretchen isn't at school the next day. Violet hangs out with Alison. The school is still buzzing about "the incident," and phones get passed around with a video posted on YouTube. I even feel kind of sorry for Gretchen. *Kind of.*

On Friday morning, Mom's weekly blog post goes live. The title this week is "The Single Mom's Guide to Dating." It's horrible and cringeworthy, but at least it isn't about me. Gretchen is back at school, her hair newly cut and her nails done in a perfect French manicure, acting for all the world like nothing happened.

At lunchtime, I watch from a distance as Violet talks and laughs with Gretchen, Alison, and Nick as if they've been friends forever. Violet has chosen them. Now, the most I can hope for is that she forgets that I, and the Secret Cooking Club, ever existed.

After school I go to the library again—this time I've got an essay to write that I actually need to do some research for. I stay until it closes. I wander home slowly, dreading the evening ahead, the weekend and, pretty much, the rest of my life.

It's almost dark by the time I get to my street. I stop outside Mrs. Simpson's house. The curtains are pulled, but I can just make out a sliver of light coming from inside. I creep up to the door and peek through the mailbox. The light is coming from the partly open kitchen door. And then I hear laughter—girls' laughter.

My heart jumps to my throat. Violet is inside. And she's with someone else—not one person, but two. "Yummy!" a high voice squeals. I know that voice.

Gretchen.

I stand there frozen, unable to breathe. I'm not sure how much time goes by, but pretty soon I see the silhouettes of Gretchen and Alison against the cozy rectangle of light from the kitchen. I hear a chorus of voices saying "bye," "thanks," and "see you later." I rush away from the door and hide behind a smelly trash can in the alleyway at the side of the house. The door opens and closes. Footsteps.

"That was actually fun." A voice—Alison's.

"Yeah, I told you Violet was cool."

My heart is thumping so loud I barely hear them walking off down the street. Whatever they were doing, Violet's stayed behind to clean up the mess. I storm up to the door and ring the bell. I hope it scares the pants off her.

There's no answer, so I kick away the mat, pick up the key, and turn it roughly in the lock. I slam the door behind me as I go inside.

There's a sound in the kitchen of running footsteps. Violet must be trying to hide. I stomp in—let her think it's Mr. Kruffs.

"Violet?" Instead of sounding menacing, my voice breaks.

There's no answer.

"How could you *do* it? We had a secret—together. How could you tell Gretchen, of all people?" My voice catches again, and an instant later, I'm sobbing. "I *trusted* you!"

Violet comes out from around the side of the bookcase. Her face seems thinner, and her eyes have dark circles underneath, like she hasn't slept.

"You said you didn't want to do this anymore," she says quietly. "I came here yesterday after school *and* the day before and waited for you. But you didn't come."

"So instead you brought Gretchen! You know how I feel about her. You brought her *here*!" The words gurgle from my mouth like poison. "You betrayed me, Violet. You betrayed us."

"No, I didn't." She tries to put her hand on my arm, but I jerk away. It's then that I notice the tray of undecorated cupcakes in frilly pink wrappings sitting on a wire rack to cool. I clench my fists to keep from throwing them in the trash.

"Gretchen figured out it was me," Violet blurts. "That I was involved in the Secret Cooking Club. I mean, it was kind of obvious, wasn't it? The free samples started just about the time I joined the school."

"So? You could have denied it."

"No, I couldn't! Nick saw you in the hallway acting weird. Gretchen put two and two together, and figured out that you put the pies in the cafeteria."

"No!" I put my hands over my face. "That's exactly what I was afraid of."

"Listen, okay? She thought the Secret Cooking Club was a really cool idea. She tried the oatmeal bars and loved them. And she didn't get sick from the banoffee pie—she had a stomach virus."

"That's ridiculous."

"I didn't know what to do. The secret was out. I knew you wouldn't want her to tell your mom."

"My mom?" My whole body goes rigid.

"Yeah," Violet says. "So to make her keep the secret, I invited her and Alison to join." Her shoulders slump. "I saw where the key was kept so I knew I could get in… I realize now it was a huge mistake, but I didn't know what else to do. I figured you probably hated me for making you put the pies in the cafeteria. But even if you never came back, I wanted to keep the secret. I told Gretchen she could never tell anyone that you

were involved. That you hated what she did to you before. I…"
Her voice quavers. "I thought I was doing you a favor…"

"A favor!" I cry. "Is that what you call it? I poured out
my heart to you—told you all about my stupid mom and how
she makes me feel. And what do you do? Tell *Gretchen*, of
all people!"

"I'm sorry, Scarlett."

"I mean, how would you like it if your mom splashed your
whole life over the internet? How would you like it if your
mom were like mine—?"

I stop abruptly. Violet turns away, her shoulders shaking
as she begins to cry. All of a sudden, it hits me. I've made a
terrible mistake.

CHAPTER 21

Buttercream

MY ANGER DISSOLVES IN MY throat. Now it makes a kind of sad, tragic sense. For all my whining about my mom, Violet has never mentioned hers. And I've never asked. Aunt Hilda— why is Violet *living* with Aunt Hilda?

"My mom's dead," Violet says. "So's my dad. So, you're right—I don't know exactly how you feel."

"Oh, Violet." I take a step backward, stunned by the force of her revelation and, unwittingly, my own selfishness. She lifts her head, and I come up and put my arm over her shoulders. "I'm so sorry," I say.

Nodding, she wipes her eyes. I sit her down in one of the chairs. The cupcakes are in front of us. I lean forward and examine them. Even without icing, they look fluffy and delicious.

"Do you want to talk about it?" I say quietly.

She doesn't answer. Next to the cupcakes is a big bowl with a wooden spoon sticking out of it. She pulls the bowl in front of her and starts stirring—it's the icing for the cupcakes. A piping bag and a box of cake-decorating nozzles are sitting on the table.

"We made these cupcakes for my birthday," Violet explains. "It's tomorrow." Her lip quivers. "I felt bad coming here without you, but I really thought you'd quit. I didn't want to lose this." She gestures with the spoon. "The Secret Cooking Club was important to me too."

"I've been totally selfish," I say. "And I hope you can forgive me."

She smiles faintly. "Of course."

"Can I help with the cupcakes?"

"Yeah."

We split the icing into two separate bowls. I color my half pink, and she adds clear white glitter to hers. I hand her the icing package. The picture on the box shows that you can make little whirls and swirls with the icing bag. It looks kind of complicated, but I'm sure Violet can do it. She spoons some glitter icing into the bag and tries out some of the nozzles on a paper towel. I smooth on a base layer of pink to each cupcake.

She takes one of the cupcakes I iced and begins making a little border of icing swirls around the edge. Then she puts a crystallized violet in the middle and surrounds it with crystallized rose petals. Finally, she tops it all off by sprinkling on pink edible glitter.

"It's so pretty," I say.

"I love doing the piping."

I hand her another cupcake. She changes nozzles and this time she makes a border like a ribbon. We work in silence for a few minutes.

"My parents were in a car accident," she says finally. "They were driving home from a church fund-raiser and a drunk driver hit them head-on. Dad was killed immediately. But Mom…" She sniffs. A tear trickles down her cheek. She stops piping the cupcakes and wipes her sleeve across her face. "They thought she would be okay. She was in a coma. I moved in with Aunt Hilda and visited Mom every day in the hospital and sat with her for hours. I talked to her, sang songs—stuff like that. I just wanted to do something to make her wake up." She swallows hard. "And then she did wake up. She didn't know who I was. They said she had trauma to her brain and internal organs, but that in time she might recover. But as I was sitting there, the machine started beeping.

She went into cardiac arrest. They did what they could, but nothing worked."

"I'm so sorry." As I say it again, I realize that *sorry* has to be the most useless word in the whole world. "It must have been...I mean, so awful."

She picks up the icing bag again. "It was," she says. "I try not to think about it. But sometimes, I dream about that sound—when she flatlined." Another tear dribbles down her face. She wipes it away quickly. "I don't usually cry."

"It's okay—really." I give her another quick hug. "And I'm so sorry I've been whining about my mom, when at least she's—" I stop, worried that I've put my foot in my mouth again.

"...alive," Violet finishes for me. "Don't worry about it." She starts on the next cupcake. "Your mom sounds pretty awful. I guess I'm lucky—Aunt Hilda's been really nice to me." Her hand trembles, and she blurs the border she's making. I smooth it over with a knife so she can start again. "But she'll never be Mom."

"Yeah," I say stupidly. I remember the pang—the very brief pang—I felt when I saw the ambulance in our street and worried that maybe something had happened to Mom. When Dad left, I felt sad, and for a while I wondered if there was something I could have done to be a better daughter so he would have stayed. But Dad had nearly always been at work or out with his friends; he'd never had much time for Kelsie and me, so it wasn't such a big change when he suddenly wasn't there. Kelsie was only a toddler, so she barely even remembers him. But if something happened to Mom…

I shiver inwardly. She may not be perfect—far from it—but she's still my mom.

"Aunt Hilda had to take me because there was no one else. I don't think she really wanted to—I mean, she has her own life. She likes to go out with her friends after work, but she doesn't want to leave me alone. Plus, she got divorced a year or so ago, and she joined an internet dating site. I'm…you know…kind of in the way."

"I'm sure that's not true."

She shrugs. "Whatever. At least I've got this." She points to the cupcakes that look so beautifully white, pink, and sparkly.

"Yeah."

She looks up at me, her eyes the color of a day-old bruise. "So now you know. My life in a nutshell."

I nod.

"Well, what do we do now?" she says. "About the Secret Cooking Club? I need to know… Are you still in?"

"Yeah," I say immediately. "I'm still in."

I'm still in.

Of course I am. Violet needs a friend as much as I do, and besides, the Secret Cooking Club is half me. Or…a quarter, now.

I lie awake in bed that night, unable to sleep. I still feel worried that Violet let Gretchen in on our secret—even if she meant well. When we'd finished the cupcakes and were cleaning up the kitchen, Violet assured me Gretchen was totally on board and would keep things a secret. Alison wasn't a problem—she would do whatever Gretchen told her. She said she'd talk to Gretchen and Alison tomorrow, and we could all meet up on Sunday.

"Okay," I said, still skeptical. "But if Gretchen tells anyone, then that's it, I'm out," I warned. "Do you understand?"

Violet said she understood. She said she would take care of everything.

I have to believe her.

CHAPTER 22

The New Secret Cooking Club

"WELCOME TO THE SECRET COOKING Club." My voice comes out less steady than when I practiced it. I force a smile as Violet comes into Mrs. Simpson's kitchen followed by Gretchen and Alison.

Gretchen eyes me carefully. "Hello, Scarlett."

"This is such a killer kitchen," Alison says. "It must be nice to have a superblogger for a mom."

I glance over at Violet. She's obviously not told them whose kitchen this really is. She shrugs awkwardly.

"We need to get a few ground rules straight." I gesture to the table where I've set out some mugs and glasses. The kettle has boiled, and I've also set out a carton of juice. Alison and Violet sit, but Gretchen leans against the shelves of cookbooks, her arms crossed.

I'm not quite sure what to do next: sit or stand; pour drinks or not. There's a strong current of tension in the room. I continue standing at the head of the table and just keep talking.

"First of all," I say, "secret means secret." I look squarely at Gretchen.

She lifts her chin as though I've insulted her, staring right back. "We won't tell anyone at school," she says. "If that's what you're worried about."

"Or my mom?" I realize I've given away my entire hand in three words, but what else can I do?

She pauses long enough to make me sweat. "Or your mom."

Our eyes lock for a long second. I decide enough is enough. I sit down at the table. I'm not sure which one of us has won, but the tension begins to ebb away. Gretchen makes herself a cup of hot chocolate, and I pour juice into glasses for the rest of us.

"Okay," I say. "That's the main thing. But there are still some other things you should know." I look at Alison. "Like… this isn't my house."

Violet gets the cupcakes we left here out of the fridge while I explain about Mrs. Simpson. Gretchen tries not to act surprised, but I'm sure I see a new respect dawning in her eyes. I tell them about my breaking and entering to feed the cat, and how Violet and I visited Mrs. Simpson in the hospital.

When I'm finished, I expect some kind of reaction—questions or something. But by then, we're all biting into the delicious, pink cakes with buttercream swirls, and no one says much of anything at all. Finally, Alison wipes her mouth. "You can trust us, Scarlett. I mean, the whole thing is cool because it's a secret."

"And since we're a club," Gretchen says, "we should have some kind of secret handshake or password."

"Okay," I acknowledge.

"How about 'banoffee'?" Violet suggests.

Gretchen makes a face.

"Maybe not." Alison laughs.

"What about 'marzipan'?" Violet tries again.

"Too complicated," Gretchen says.

"'Buttercream,'" I say quietly.

"What's that?"

"'Buttercream.'"

Gretchen looks at Violet, who nods. "Yeah," Gretchen says. "That sounds good."

"Fine," Alison says. "Now that we've got that over with, are we going to cook something, or what? Those free samples aren't going to make themselves."

I get up from the table and retrieve the little marble-covered notebook from the book stand. "This is the recipe book we've been using," I say. "It's really special—at least, I think so."

Violet nods.

I hand it to Gretchen as if it were a flag of truce. "What do you guys feel like making?"

Gretchen and Alison flip through the book. "I can't believe someone took so much time to write all of this," Alison says. "And the pictures—they're so cute! Let's try the Knave of Hearts Strawberry Tarts."

"I'd rather do Hansel and Gretel's Gingerbread," Gretchen says. She lowers her voice as if someone might leak her preference to the PTA. "Gingerbread is my favorite."

Leaving them to get started, I check what's in the cupboards and the fridge. To my surprise—why am I surprised by anything that happens in Rosemary's Kitchen?—there's lots of fresh fruit in the fridge, including cartons of strawberries and blueberries, kiwis, and even a little basket of cherries.

"I think we should start with fruit tarts," I say. "We can do gingerbread next time." I glance at Gretchen to make sure she's okay with that.

"Fine." She shrugs. "Whatever."

I take the fruit out of the fridge. Violet looks surprised too, but like me, she just goes with it.

"Okay," I say, "now, first, everyone wash their hands. Then, someone needs to wash and cut the fruit, someone needs to make the custard, and someone needs to make the pastry for the tarts, and... Oh, before I forget, we need to preheat the oven."

The tasks get easily assigned. I team up with Gretchen to make the pastry dough. Together we find the ingredients and measure them into a bowl.

"Did your mom teach you to cook?" Gretchen asks me.

"No," I say. "She doesn't cook at all really. She doesn't have time."

Gretchen stiffens, and I wonder what I've said.

"I mean, she's too busy making fun of me," I add.

She stops measuring. "I never really got why you were so angry. Your mom made you into a star." She frowns. "And then, you completely changed. It was as if you didn't have time for any of your friends, or anything at school anymore."

"That's totally not it." How could Gretchen, of all people, get things so wrong?

"Well, what then?"

I tip the flour into the bowl. "You know, before she started, I thought I was pretty normal. I sometimes did stuff I wasn't proud of...you know, embarrassing stuff. But it didn't seem like a big deal. But then, Mom started broadcasting every-thing. It was front-page news that I farted at Christmas dinner and scratched my eczema in my sleep. And she'd go on about what underwear I wore and what my gym clothes smelled like. Suddenly, all that stuff seemed huge—it was all I could think about. I felt like everyone was looking at me and laughing." I shove the bowl toward Gretchen. "I mean, do you really think that makes me a star? Do you think I didn't have time for any of my friends so I could get more of that?"

Gretchen shrugs. "To be honest, I didn't know what to think. I mean, you totally helped on my campaign, and then you disappeared as soon as I won. I thought maybe you were jealous—but then, why didn't you just run yourself? You totally could have won."

"Me?"

"I mean, you were cool! Smart and talkative and stuff. Everybody thought so."

"I thought I was the 'most boring girl in the world'—your words, not mine."

"Come on, Scarlett, I didn't really mean that. I was fed up, that's all. You never even said congratulations when I won. I had no idea what I'd done wrong."

"Well, emailing my mom didn't help."

Gretchen puts her hands on her hips. "I thought your mom was totally cool when she started that blog. And for the record, she emailed me, not the other way around. I am the PTA rep after all. She asked me stuff about you because you stopped talking to her. I assumed she was just worried. I said maybe you weren't feeling well because it was your time of the month or something. I had no idea she was going to start writing about it."

"So it was all a misunderstanding?"

"Maybe."

I add the cubed butter and stir it in. I stop waiting for an apology that isn't going to come, and wonder if maybe I should be the one to say sorry. Maybe I was a little quick to drop her as a friend—just the way Stacie did to me. Maybe I should have tried to tell her how I felt six months ago. Maybe, maybe. But *maybe* it isn't too late.

I stand back and let Gretchen rub the butter into the flour. "I'm glad you won the election," I say. "And I'm glad you're here now."

"Yeah," she says.

"It's just…the mom stuff has been awful for me. Before the blog, I guess Mom and I did get along—or at least, we were kind of normal. But now, it's 'Help! My Daughter This' and 'Psst! My Daughter That.' All I know is—she can't find out about this."

"She won't find out from me." Gretchen pauses for a long second. "I promise."

"Okay." I hope I'm not foolish to believe her.

I close my eyes and take a bite of fruit tart. My tongue tingles at the different tastes: the pastry light and crumbly, the custard rich and wobbly, and the fruit shiny and fresh (arranged neatly by Violet) on top and covered in a sticky apricot glaze. By the time we finish up for the evening, the four of us are kind of normal together. I have to admit that four people seems more like a real club than just Violet and me. I'm relieved when Gretchen volunteers to put the fruit tarts in the cafeteria at lunchtime. ("Well, no one will think *I'm* involved, will they?" she says.)

Once the fruit tarts have been put away, Violet, Gretchen, and I clean up the kitchen (Alison manages to spend most of the clean-up time answering texts). We double-check that we've left no trace we were ever here, and when it's time to leave, I lock the door and replace the key under the mat. Then we all repeat the secret password: "Buttercream."

· CHAPTER 23 ·

Too Good to Be True

THINGS CAN'T BE GOING THIS well. I mean, this is my life after all. The next day, everything proceeds without a hitch. Gretchen and Alison say hi to me in the hallway, but that's it—acting friendly but not too friendly. Violet smiles at me from across the room as usual. Gretchen volunteers to help the teacher photocopy something, so she doesn't even need the bathroom pass. And in the cafeteria at lunchtime, there are no fights or vomiting. Everyone lines up and gets their piece of fruit tart, and makes "mmm-ing" noises and whispers how awesome it is, and how cool the Secret Cooking Club is. Best of all, Nick Farr still seems to be a fan. I join the line for a slice of fruit tart, and overhear him saying something to Gretchen. "You know, I wish I knew how to cook stuff like this."

For a split second, I have a little fantasy—that all the noise in the room hushes up, and everything goes into slow motion. Then, the universe is just me and him. I boldly walk up, tap him on the shoulder, and say, "Why don't you join us?"

But of course, I don't.

Instead, I try to be happy that Nick Farr and everyone else seem to like the fruit tarts and respect the club Violet and I started, even if they'll never know I'm involved. Or so I hope, anyway.

Because when lunch is over and things are back to normal, I'm aware of a nagging feeling in the pit of my stomach that won't go away. To quote one of my mom's favorite sayings in her blog: "Things that seem too good to be true usually are."

After school, the four of us meet up at Mrs. Simpson's house. We all say the password "buttercream" on our way in, giggling a little at how silly it is to have a password. Everything is the same as when we left it the previous night. Gretchen and Violet are talking about how much everyone liked the tarts. Alison gets the little recipe book off its stand and starts flipping through it.

I leave the kitchen to lock the front door—I'd forgotten

to do it when we came in. A hear what sounds like a van idling outside. I can't see anything through the stained-glass panel in the door, but I have the same strange feeling I had earlier—this can't last. My heart thumps in my chest.

The others are laughing and talking loudly in the kitchen. I'm about to go and rejoin them when I hear a voice outside the door. "You sure you can manage until the nurse comes tomorrow? I'm happy to help you inside."

And then the shrill reply of a woman's voice. "Nonsense. I don't need anyone to help me do anything now that I'm home. You can send your nurse if you like, but I won't let her in!" A key turns in the lock.

I stand there, paralyzed. The door opens and I'm face-to-face with an old woman: Rosemary Simpson.

She takes one look at me and lets out a strangled cry of surprise.

"Mrs. Simpson, please—it's okay!" I rush forward and try to help her inside. Her hair is like wire escaping from a bun at her neck, and she's leaning heavily on a cane.

"Who are you? What are you doing here?" She holds up the cane with a gnarled hand and waves it at me. "Shoo…"

I step back to avoid the random swinging and hold up my hands. I'm aware of the others just behind me, peeking out of the kitchen door. "I'm Scarlett," I blurt out. "Your neighbor. I, uh…I've been feeding your cat."

Her eyes are bloodshot and wild. "Treacle? Where's Treacle? What have you done with him?"

"Nothing," I say. "The cat…Treacle? He hasn't been here the last few days. But I came over to check if it—he—is back."

"Treacle?" she calls out, craning her neck to look for him.

"He isn't here."

She whirls back on me. I cower another few steps backward.

Violet comes up to my side. "Hi, Mrs. Simpson," she says, "would you like a cup of tea? We've got cupcakes left over from my birthday too. With buttercream icing and sparkles. They're really nice."

The old woman blinks and leans forward. Her wrinkled face goes white, almost as if she's seen a ghost. "Cupcakes?" she says. "Buttercream?" She stares at the room around her like she's trying to figure out where she is. Her eyes settle on Violet. "Yes, I'll try one." She hobbles toward the kitchen. "And tea with two sugars and a dollop of milk."

Gretchen and Alison make a quick retreat and start setting out cups and the last of the cupcakes on a plate. Violet sticks close to Mrs. Simpson's side, pulling up a chair for her.

Alison puts the plate of cupcakes in front of the old woman, and Gretchen makes her a cup of tea. I stand well back out of the way. It's like the four of us are all holding our breath. Mrs. Simpson lifts the cupcake in her trembling fingers, holds it to her nose, and sniffs it. She closely inspects the icing swirls, the pink glitter, and the flower made of crystallized violets and rose petals in the center. For a moment, she frowns. Then she takes a bite.

It seems to take forever as she chews the cake with a clack of false teeth, and then swallows. I feel as though I'm on national television, waiting for the all-important verdict of the judges on *Cake Wars*. Using her cane as a pivot, she swivels around in her chair and looks straight at me.

"You," she says, pointing a wizened finger. "You did this?"

My mouth goes dry as I try to speak. "You're right, Mrs. Simpson. I started this. We shouldn't be here—I know that. And I'm sorry. We'll leave now and never come back. Or...you can call my mom if you want. Please don't get my friends in trouble. It's all my fault, not theirs."

"No," Violet says, "that's not true. We all did it. It's all of our faults."

"Hush!" Mrs. Simpson doesn't turn around, but keeps staring at me. "This tastes as though it has two teaspoons of baking powder in it. It should only have one. Don't they teach you girls any math these days?"

"Um...I thought I put in one," Gretchen says. "I must have made a mistake."

"And the buttercream is too solid." She turns to Violet. "You should have used a dash more milk. And a hint of vanilla, I think." She licks her wrinkled lips. "Other than that...it's passable."

"Passable?"

She turns away from me back to the others. "You've shown that you can follow a recipe." Her voice takes on a lecturing tone. "You can stir things together, put it in a pan, and stick it in the oven." She *tsks*. "And by the way, the oatmeal bars you brought me were underbaked in the middle. You should have cooked them longer at a lower heat." Her hawk-like gaze turns to Violet. "And the crystallized violets were an interesting twist, but they made the whole thing too sweet. The bottom line is that you've found my kitchen and had your fun experimenting with your pastries and desserts. But now..." She crosses her arms.

The word seems to echo around the room.

I bite my lip. She's going to tell us to leave—

"...now, you need to learn how to cook."

· CHAPTER 24 ·

Stick to the Ribs

GONE ARE THE CUPCAKES AND banoffee pie; the oatmeal bars and fruit tarts are a dim and distant memory. Mrs. Simpson says we need to learn how to cook for real, and she isn't kidding.

"You can't think you know how to cook just because you can whip up a few desserts." She gazes at each of us, her sunken blue eyes twinkling. "You girls these days are too skinny. In my day, we had rationing because of the war." She shakes her head like the memory hurts. "There was no sugar and no sweets. We all learned how to cook food that 'sticks to the ribs.'"

I nod politely. Suddenly, I'm very hungry for real food.

She flips the pages of the notebook, pausing and considering.

"Do you know what I craved the most as a girl?" Mrs. Simpson says, her bushy eyebrows raised.

We shake our heads.

"Eggs. That's what. Real eggs, perfectly cooked, and everything that goes with them. But all we had back then were powdered eggs. You don't know how lucky you are." She purses her lips. "Now I use only the freshest of ingredients— that's one of the secrets of being a good cook."

"Is that the secret ingredient?" I ask shyly.

"No." My question seems to startle her. "Not that." Her eyes suddenly appear glassy and far away. "That's something else entirely."

For a long moment I worry that I've spoiled everything. I look at the floor, hardly daring to breathe.

"So, we'll start with this one." Recovering, she props open the recipe book on the stand. Relief flows through me. The recipe on the page is for Chicken Licken's Eggs Benedict. "If you can't cook an egg properly, then you may as well get out of the kitchen."

The four of us go through a whole dozen eggs, cracking them into cups, before Mrs. Simpson is even halfway satisfied with our egg-breaking technique. Even Gretchen is sweating by the time we end up with a load of eggs in cups ready to poach. Mrs.

Simpson assigns Gretchen to do the poaching and prepare the sliced ham, Violet and Alison to bake the muffins, and me to make the hollandaise sauce.

While Mrs. Simpson is helping Gretchen get the equipment out of the cupboards, I turn to Violet. "Looks like we have another new member."

"It's all a little weird, isn't it?" Violet keeps her voice low.

"What?"

"That she'd just let us stay and keep on cooking."

I shrug. "Maybe it was the oatmeal bars."

"Or she's just lonely," Alison says. Flour puffs everywhere as she tips it into the bowl.

"Anyway," I say, "let's just go with it for now."

It's as if we're under a spell. An hour goes by, then another. Nothing else seems to matter—if we're expected at home or have homework or had other plans. The muffins bake, the hollandaise sauce gets whisked up and made. Mrs. Simpson tells us stories about how people cooked during the war, and about how when she was a girl, they didn't have supermarkets or microwave-ready meals or anything like that. While she mostly lets us continue with following the recipe, occasionally she cackles the odd instruction or bangs her stick against the floor to make a point. The four of us scurry around like old-time kitchen maids.

Somehow we manage to finish making the eggs Benedict. My stomach is rumbling because it's almost eight o'clock and none of us have eaten anything. Violet stacks everything on the plates: muffin, ham, egg, and a little swirl of hollandaise sauce for decoration. The four of us sneak glances at each other as Mrs. Simpson sits at the table and cuts a piece of what we've made. I think we're all holding our breath—I know I am.

She raises the fork to her lips and pops the bite into her mouth. She chews slowly and deliberately, the skin on her neck wobbling as she finally swallows it.

Then she looks up. "Well," she says, waving an exasperated hand, "don't just stand there staring. Sit down and eat."

The other three scramble to sit at the table, but I stand there, my hands on my hips. "But aren't you going to say if it's any good?"

She slowly turns to look at me, still chewing. She pats her lips with a napkin and takes a sip of tea.

"You cooked it," she says. "Only you can say for sure."

"Oh," I say, not really understanding.

I sit at the table. My friends and I silently lift our knives and forks, as if taking the first bite is some kind of test. I cut a piece off the little tower of eggs and muffin and stick it in my mouth. The tastes are wholesome and familiar, yet new at the

. It strikes me that I've never really paid attention

vhat I eat—the different flavors and textures. Maybe
part of learning how to cook is learning how to eat. I look up
and notice that Mrs. Simpson is watching *me* chew the first
bite. Her lips pursed in a thin line, she nods almost impercep-
tibly at me. I smile at my plate. I know it's good.

In no time at all, everyone's plate is completely empty.
My only regret is that we didn't make more. "Should we start
the washing up?" I ask Mrs. Simpson.

"First, let's talk about what we cooked tonight and what
we learned."

She goes around the table, asking each of us in turn what
we thought of the dish we made. Alison says that it tasted good,
and Violet says that it was fun to make. But Mrs. Simpson keeps
questioning us, making us talk about things like the balance of
the seasoning, the texture of the eggs, the crispiness of the
muffins. Gretchen thought the sauce was a little runny; Violet
thought her muffin was too brown on the bottom. When it gets
to be my turn, I don't quite know what to say.

"I thought that everything we used went really well
together," I muster finally. "Like it belonged that way all along."

For the first time all evening, Mrs. Simpson manages a
little smile. The years melt off her face. I smile back, glad to

have given a right answer. "In that case," she says, "I think we're done here. Now, get started. I want this kitchen sparkling before you leave."

"Yes, Mrs. Simpson," we all say in unison.

We jump up from the table and start a marathon of washing dishes, cleaning countertops, putting away ingredients, and wiping down the stove. I keep stealing glances at Mrs. Simpson as she drinks another cup of tea, wondering about her. Tonight she's made me think about cooking in a whole new way. And I feel good inside about what I've accomplished. That's the best part.

But by the time I finish drying the dishes, Mrs. Simpson's eyes are closed and her head is drooping. Her grip loosens on her stick, and it falls to the floor with a thud.

"We have to get her to bed," I say. We take off our aprons and help Mrs. Simpson to the sofa in the front room. We cover her with an orange knitted throw. Less than a minute later, she's asleep. All of a sudden I realize how irresponsible we've been—it must have been a shock for her to come home from the hospital, only to find a cooking club in her kitchen. We should have gone home hours ago.

"Can we just leave her?" I say to Gretchen. Together we loosen the old woman's shoes.

"I'm not sure we have much choice. I guess she'll be okay if she's asleep."

"Uh-oh!" Alison looks at the screen of her phone for the first time all evening. "I told my mom that I'd be home by 8:30 from your house, Gretch. And now it's almost 9:30. And I was supposed to finish that stupid essay."

Gretchen shrugs. "We're all in the same boat."

"Where's her stick?" I say. "She'll need it when she wakes up."

"Still in the kitchen, I guess," Violet says.

"I'll go and get it."

I head back to the kitchen. The little recipe notebook is closed on the rack, like it's resting for the night. The plates and dishes that we used have been washed and are drying on the dish rack. The pots and pans are drying at the back of the stove. There's a faint hissing sound as though a faucet is running somewhere. I check the kitchen faucet—it's off. One of the wet dish towels is crumpled up on the counter. I hang it up over the front of the stove to dry faster. I pick up Mrs. Simpson's stick and take it into the front room, propping it against the sofa so she can't miss it.

"Let's go," I say. "I'll come back tomorrow morning and check that she's okay."

We all grab our backpacks and head out the door. We're in such a hurry that no one even thinks to give the secret password.

Maybe that's what we did wrong.

· CHAPTER 25 ·

Ketchup Sky

THERE'S A LIGHT ON UNDER the door to the Mom Cave when I get back home. I tiptoe out of the kitchen toward the stairs when all of a sudden Mom bursts out.

"Scarlett! Where have you been? I've been so worried." She engulfs me in her special stale-smelling Mom hug. "I was about to call the police. I can't believe you did this to me *again*."

I'm so tired that I just stand there letting her squeeze me.

"Sorry, Mom," I say. "But I did tell you about the science project. We're working in pairs to build"—I scratch my head, trying to remember what we've done in science class this year—"a solar-powered car."

"Really?" Mom looks disappointed—she won't get much mileage out of that in her blog.

"I'm paired up with the new girl. Her name is Violet."

Mom steps back. I have to catch myself from slumping. "All right, maybe you did mention it before—I don't remember." She shrugs dismissively. "But I think it's time we got you a phone. Just so you can let me know where you are."

"A phone? Really? That would be great." Mom's always been against girls my age having phones or tablets—anything like that. While I've got her old laptop computer and printer to do my homework, she won't even let me have internet access. She's already done a post on: "We Didn't Have Any of That Stuff in My Day…So You Don't Need It Either."

"I really was worried, Scarlett. I hope you know that."

I nod, wishing I could say more—tell her I'm grateful she was worried about me. But the words won't come out.

"It's just…there's something strange with this house sometimes." She stares at the wall, oddly distracted. "It's like, I keep smelling things. And remembering…"

"Really?" I say. "Like what?"

"Never mind." She shakes her head. "I've got to get back to work now." She goes to her office door. "And because you gave me a scare, you're grounded."

Grounded! I try to protest, but she slams the door of the Mom Cave in my face. This is the first time she's ever grounded me, and I can just imagine her sitting gleefully at her computer and typing up a new blog entry: "A Mom's Pop Quiz: How Many Years Has My Daughter Taken Off My Life?"

But as long as she doesn't know about the Secret Cooking Club, I can live with whatever garbage she writes. Since we started the club, I'm stronger somehow, more confident. More like my old self.

I go upstairs and brush my teeth. I can't remember ever being so happy to flop onto my own bed. I pull the duvet up to my neck and close my eyes. But sleep doesn't come. I go back over the events of the night: from Rosemary Simpson's surprise arrival, to the egg dish that we made, to how full my stomach feels after eating something fresh and healthy. But something's nagging at the back of my mind and it won't go away. A hissing sound—as though a faucet is running somewhere…

"Wake up, Scarlett!"

A hand is shaking me in the dark, and I open my eyes. There's a strange reddish-orange glow outside the curtains, and something smells funny.

"The sky is ketchup," Kelsie says. She pulls the duvet off me. "Come and see."

I swing out of bed with a sleepy groan. The blood rushes from my head. Something is very wrong.

"Girls!" Mom's voice is frantic as she runs up the stairs. "We need to get outside right now. Something's on fire."

On fire!

All of a sudden I hear the scream of a siren rushing down the street. The ketchup sky begins to flash with the glow of the spinning light on the fire engine.

"Mrs. Simpson!" I cry. "She's in there."

"Who?" Mom barks.

"Our neighbor! She's just come home from the hospital."

We rush outside the front door. A small crowd of neighbors has gathered across the street.

Firefighters pour out of the shiny, red truck—there's at least six of them—and go up to Mrs. Simpson's front door. One of them tries the door and another one gets ready to bash it in.

"There's a key under the doormat," I yell, rushing forward. "You don't need to break down the door."

One of the firefighters gets the key and unlocks the door.

"Please step back," another one says to me. "Across the street at the very least."

"Scarlett?" Mom's voice warns. "Come here now." She

pulls me along by the arm, her other hand herding Kelsie. When we're across the street I turn back, petrified, as the fireman pushes open the door. But there's no billowing cloud of smoke: just an old woman's frightened cry: "Who are you, young man? Go away now. Shoo..."

Two more firefighters hurry in, one carrying a full-length stretcher. Mrs. Simpson's protests grow even louder. "This is my house—and I'm not leaving!"

The remaining firefighters go inside, dragging along a limp fire hose. I hear a loud crash of glass. "Please, lady!" A man's voice. "We're trying to help you. There's a fire in your kitchen."

Mom is busy trying to get Kelsie to take her thumb out of her mouth. Sensing my chance, I run back across the street. One of the neighbors calls out, and then Mom yells, "Stop, Scarlett," but I keep going. Mrs. Simpson knows me—I can help get her out of the burning house.

But just as my foot hits the curb, a sleek, black Mercedes pulls up. I stop. A man jumps out of the car: tall with a high forehead, thin nose, and slicked-back dark hair. He's wearing an expensive, black suit and shiny, black shoes. He turns to the crowd and waves briefly. Then he strides past me and up to the door.

"Aunt Rosemary?" he calls out loudly. Water begins to whoosh through the hose.

"No!" Mrs. Simpson's voice. "Turn off that water right now!"

Mr. Black Mercedes must be the nephew, Mr. Kruffs. Somehow, I'd pictured him as different—shorter, rounder, more like a fluffy poodle at a dog show. But this man looks more like a slick, modern version of a politician. Not someone I'd like to mess with.

A moment later, the two firefighters come outside with Mrs. Simpson between them—kicking and dragging her feet like a criminal resisting arrest. Mr. Kruffs makes a big show of trying to take his aunt's arm. He waves to the crowd that everything's okay—obviously playing up the politician-rescues-old-lady-from-burning-building angle. Several people take pictures with their phones.

Mrs. Simpson jerks her arm away. "You can go now, Emory," she says. "Everything is fine."

"Fine?" His voice is low. "Your house is burning down—with you in it."

"Well..." Mrs. Simpson yanks her stick away from one of the firefighters. "These men have everything taken care of. And it was only a very *small* fire." She turns to the crowd across the street and waves her cane. "Go away—shoo!"

I step forward. "Mrs. Simpson?" I try to sound calm and soothing. "Are you okay? Can I help?"

Mr. Kruffs gives me an intense glare down his long nose, as though I've just thrown an egg at his car. "Who are you?"

I stand my ground. "I'm her neighbor."

"Well, go back across the street, please. It's not safe for kids here."

Mrs. Simpson stares at me with pleading blue eyes. "Scarlett?" she says, sounding confused.

"That's right, Mrs. Simpson." Ignoring Mr. Kruffs, I reach forward and take her arm gently. "Do you want to go and wait across the street until this is over?"

The old woman looks at her nephew, hesitating. Before she can make up her mind, one of the firefighters comes out.

"Everything is under control," he says, loud enough for the crowd to hear. "You can all go back to bed."

Someone chuckles like he's said something funny. No one leaves. I glance over at Mom, who's talking to a woman from down the street. I catch a snippet about Superdrug and the Mom Survival Kit.

Mr. Kruffs steps up and stands next to the firefighter. "Everything is going to be fine now." He grins widely as a few more photos are snapped. "I think we should all get out of the way now and let our brave firefighters finish doing their jobs."

The crowd murmurs, and a few people begin to leave.

I lean closer to Mrs. Simpson and listen as the firefighter speaks to Mr. Kruffs. "It was just a small, contained fire," he says. "The stove in the kitchen was left on and a dish towel caught fire."

"A dish towel…" My hand flies to my mouth. *What have I done?*

The firefighter continues talking to Mr. Kruffs. "There's some smoke damage, a burnt window frame, and a broken window. It could have been a lot worse."

But things *are* worse. I know that as soon as I look at Mr. Kruffs, his face grimacing in concern. "The stove was left on," he repeats. He shakes his head and *tsks* dramatically. "Really, Aunt Rosemary."

"It wasn't her fault!" I say. Guilt and fear churn inside me.

"Please stay out of this," Mr. Kruffs says sharply. He turns back to his aunt. "This proves that you can't keep living here on your own."

Her face crumples. "Yes, I can," she says. "And I wouldn't be on my own if you hadn't taken Treacle."

Mr. Kruffs gives a pained-looking shrug. "Shouldn't you be thanking me for that? That greedy old cat could have starved to death while you were in the hospital."

"He's not greedy," I cut in. "And he wouldn't have starved. *I* was feeding him. You should bring him back."

Mr. Kruffs stares down at me like a vulture in a tall tree. "This has nothing to do with you," he says.

Mrs. Simpson's bony hand tightens on my arm. "It's everything to do with me," I say with a sudden surge of protectiveness. "Mrs. Simpson is my neighbor—we share a wall. If her house had burnt down, so would ours." I turn to her. "Come on, Mrs. Simpson, let's go. I'll ask Mom if you can sleep at our house tonight."

"There, Emory, you see?" Rosemary Simpson gives her nephew a defiant look. She allows me to steer her away. She hobbles toward our house, leaning heavily on both me and her stick.

"I'll be back in the morning," Mr. Kruffs says. In two strides he's back at the black Mercedes and getting into the driver's seat. "We'll talk about this further. And this time, I'm going to take some action."

Mrs. Simpson's whole body starts to tremble.

"It's okay," I whisper. "It's going to be fine."

"Don't let him put me in a home, please."

"I won't, Mrs. Simpson." I bite my lip. "I promise."

CHAPTER 26

Maple Syrup

BUT HOW ON EARTH CAN I promise something like that? I'm the one who failed to notice the burner was still on. I'm the one who draped the dish towel too close. The fire was my fault, and Mrs. Simpson is paying the price! I stand next to her, feeling as though my chest might explode. Suddenly, Mom storms across the street, dragging my sister along with her. She takes my arm and pulls me aside.

"Scarlett," she scolds, "that man is a politician. You sounded very rude when you spoke to him. What's going on?"

"Mom…" I choke. *Tell her. No, don't tell her. What should I do?* I take a long breath to pull myself together. "Please can Mrs. Simpson stay at our house tonight? It sounds like the firefighters have made kind of a mess in there. She needs somewhere to go."

Mom looks at Mrs. Simpson's bent figure, then back at me. Her cheeks are red from the cold air and the effort of boring the pants off our neighbor with stories of the Superdrug product selection committee.

"Honestly, Scarlett!" she says in a harsh whisper. "We can't take someone in just like that. Where would she sleep?"

"In my bed, or on the sofa bed—I don't care."

"But we don't even know her—"

"We can't just leave her out here!" I cry. "She's our neighbor, and her house was on fire. We need to help her."

"But I've got a deadline, I'm so busy…" Mom shakes her head. "You know that, Scarlett."

I take a breath. "I do know that, Mom. You have to write your blog. What's it going to be this time? 'Help! My Teenage Daughter Is Taking in the Homeless Off the Street'? Or maybe, 'Psst! My Thoughtless Daughter Made Me Miss My Deadline.' But if you write that, I'm going to get online and be the first person to leave a comment." I stand straighter. "I'm going to tell everyone—all your precious readers, Twitter followers, and Facebook friends—that the old woman who lives next door had no place to go and you wouldn't even let her sleep on the sofa for one night." I raise my chin. "How do you think *that* will make you look at your next meeting with Superdrug?"

"You wouldn't dare," Mom spits. "If you ever do anything to hurt my reputation online, then I'll...I'll..."

"It's just for one night, Mom. Let Mrs. Simpson stay with us for one night."

Mom's eyes skewer me but I can't back down—not now. "We're not done with this conversation." She walks over to Mrs. Simpson—the old woman seems to have dozed off leaning on her stick—and puts her hand on her arm. "Mrs. Simpson?" Mom sounds as though she's talking to a child. "I'm Claire— Scarlett's mom. If you need a place to stay for tonight, you can come next door to our house."

Somehow I manage to fall asleep because when I wake up the next morning, my body feels like lead. The memories of the night come rushing back—the fire I caused, standing up to Mr. Kruffs *and* Mom, and most of all, the helpless look of trust on Mrs. Simpson's face through it all. I get out of bed and rush to the window. The fire engines are gone without any sign they were ever really here. Everything is still and quiet. I get dressed and go downstairs to check on our guest.

The blanket is folded on the sofa, and the room is empty. I feel a stab of panic. I'd offered Mrs. Simpson my bed, but she said she preferred to sleep on the sofa downstairs. What if she wandered off in the night—sleepwalking maybe—and got hit by a car? Or maybe Mr. Kruffs broke in and gagged her and took her off to a home, and I'll never know where she is or what happened, and it's all my fault—

And then I smell it. Like a zombie, I turn and leave the room in a daze. Whatever it is, it's coming from *our* kitchen—and I can already tell it's going to be delicious.

I practically collide at the bottom of the stairs with Mom. She's looks sleepy and grumpy with uncombed hair and no makeup.

"I'm sorry, Mom," I blurt out. "I shouldn't have said those things last night."

She rubs her eyes. "No, Scarlett, I was the one who was wrong. You were just trying to be kind and neighborly—the way I raised you."

I smile faintly and don't bother to contradict her.

Mom sniffs the air. "What's that? It smells like cooking."

"I think it's Mrs. Simpson's way of saying thank you."

Mom raises her eyebrows. "Oh?"

I follow her to the kitchen. Mom stops at the door and gasps. A second later, I can see why.

The kitchen is immaculate—the cleaning up is done,

the magazines and clutter neatly stacked to one side, and the table has been washed and set with four places. There are two large cast-iron pans on the stove, one filled with four sizzling eggs, and one that I can't see because Mrs. Simpson's back is blocking my view. She's standing straight and steady without any sign of her stick. A second later, she lifts the frying pan and something flips into the air. She catches it in the pan and removes it with a spatula on to a plate.

"Sit down," she says, without turning around. "Everything will be ready in about five minutes."

Mom and I look at each other wide-eyed. I wouldn't even think of not obeying the command. Mom sits at one end of the table. I sit at my usual place, and behind me I hear the shuffling feet of my sister in her bunny slippers.

"Oooh, breakfast," Kelsie says. "Smells nice."

"Yeah," I say. "Sit down."

Mrs. Simpson brings Mom a steaming cup of coffee. "Thank you," Mom says in a croaky voice. The milk and sugar are already sitting neatly in front of her. Mrs. Simpson goes back to the stove and spoons more batter into the hot pan.

"I'm not the biggest fan of cooking trends nowadays," the old woman says. "It's all nonfat this and no-carbs that. But when they do things the old-fashioned, home-cooked way, they get it right. Like pancakes and pure maple syrup. Nothing beats it if you ask me."

"I love pancakes!" my sister says. "It's like when we went to Disney World."

I smile at her. Just before Dad left, we had a family vacation in Florida. We stayed at a little motel next to an International House of Pancakes. I can almost remember how good it all tasted.

"Where did you get everything?" Mom asks, looking flustered. "I'm afraid I forgot to arrange a food delivery for this week."

"From my house," Mrs. Simpson says. "The fire really was nothing—just a little smoke damage." She smiles in my direction. "The refrigerator was fine. I went over early to make sure I saved what I could."

"Good thinking," Mom says. "And I'm glad the fire wasn't serious."

"Um," I say, biting my lip, "there's something I need to say—"

Mrs. Simpson cuts me off with a quick finger to her lips. I stop. She begins handing out the plates.

"It's just...can I help with that?" I mumble.

She waves away my offer. This is her moment.

In addition to pancakes, maple syrup, and perfectly cooked eggs, there's bacon, fruit salad, and toast with fresh strawberry jam from a jar with a handwritten label. It's like being in breakfast heaven.

When everyone else is served, Mrs. Simpson sets down her own plate, but keeps standing behind her chair. "Eat it while it's hot," she says. She watches intently as we pick up our forks and try the food. After that, no one speaks—it's all too delicious for words. Mrs. Simpson finally sits, a satisfied smile on her face. I smile too—for a second. Then I'm back to eating the best breakfast ever.

Mom gracefully ducks out after a second helping—but before doing the dishes—and Kelsie goes off to watch TV. I'm left facing Mrs. Simpson across the table.

"That was amazing," I say. "Thank you so much."

Mrs. Simpson sighs and begins clearing the plates.

I jump up. "I'll do that," I say, taking the plate from her hand and running water in the sink to do the dishes.

"No, child." She waves at me to sit back down. "I've got a headache. And when that happens, it helps to have something to focus on. I need to think straight."

I pour myself a third glass of fresh orange juice and sit. "What can I do to help you?" I say. "Violet and I—well, all of us really—we'd like to do something. Your nephew has no right to put you in a home. He just can't!"

The old woman's shoulders droop like a wilted flower.

"I mean, you didn't start that fire! We left the stove on, and I put the dish towel on the front of the oven to dry. The fire was my fault. And I'm going to tell your nephew—and my mom—the truth." I feel like a prisoner going to jail, but I know it's the right thing to do.

Mrs. Simpson straightens suddenly and turns to me. "Don't mention it to them, Scarlett," she says. "It won't help anything. If Emory knows you were there in the house, it might make things worse."

"But why? Isn't it worse if he thinks you can't look after yourself?"

She turns back to the sink and begins soaping the dishes with a sponge, pausing only to tuck a stray strand of gray hair back into her bun. "Everyone gets old," she says finally. "There's no escaping that. I have to go sometime, and I'm okay with that. I'd just like to stay in my own home as long as I can, that's all." She stops talking and turns to look at me. A tear runs down her cheek—or maybe it's a soapsud.

I stand. "How about I dry?" I offer.

Mrs. Simpson nods. I grab a dish towel, and we both do the dishes in silence. My mind is turning over and over. There must be something I can do, something the Secret Cooking Club can do. But what?

When we've finished the dishes, Mrs. Simpson dries her hands and takes off her apron. Her ankles are thick and saggy in too-dark stockings.

"I'd like my cat to be with me," she says. "If I have to go into one of *those* places."

"We need to get Treacle back anyway." I fold my arms stubbornly. "And as far as I'm concerned, you're not going anywhere if you don't want to."

Her smile is fragile. "Thank you, child. And now, I'd like to go back to my house."

"Are you sure?" Part of me was hoping Mrs. Simpson would stay here with us.

"Yes," she insists. "I have to deal with this on my own. Trust me, it's better that way." She rubs her temples as if she's in pain.

"But what about the fire? I mean, aren't you mad at us?"

She gives a little chuckle. "Let me tell you a secret, Scarlett. Everyone makes mistakes. In this case, there was no harm done, you learned something, and it will never happen again. I know that."

"Oh," I say, some of the tension draining away. "I'm sorry all the same."

"I know." She smiles.

"You'll be okay going home on your own?"

"Yes, I will." She grips her stick tightly and hobbles toward the front door. I open it and she goes outside, her stick clonking on the sidewalk. I watch to make sure she's okay. When she gets to her own front door, she stops. "By the way, Scarlett," she says.

"Yeah? I mean…yes?"

"I shall expect you and your friends at five o'clock today. Don't be late."

I stare at her in disbelief.

"Um, okay," I say. "We won't be."

Back inside my house I get Mom's phone from its charger and quickly call Violet.

"We've got a situation," I say. I tell her all about the fire, about Mrs. Simpson staying with us, about the breakfast—and about how we can't be late.

"Oh, Scarlett," Violet says, "that's so awful. I can't believe we… It's terrible!"

"I wanted to tell Mr. Kruffs, but she didn't want me to. She said it would only make things worse. But I'm not sure I believe that. We have to do something."

"And she really still wants us to come over? Didn't you say the whole kitchen was on fire?"

"No. Luckily it wasn't that bad—just some smoke damage. It could have been a lot worse apparently. But now Mr. Kruffs is trying to put her in a home."

"A home? But she has a home."

"No! I mean an old people's home. Like one of those awful places you hear about on the news. I bet there's nothing to do but sit around and watch TV and play bridge. You probably have to eat horrible mushy food so your dentures don't fall out. Everyone's pretty much just waiting to die."

"Ugh." Violet says. "She can't go there. But what can we do?"

Secretly, I'm a little disappointed Violet doesn't have a solution, because I know I don't.

"Can you call Gretchen and Alison?" I grasp at straws. "We need an emergency meeting right after school. We have to think of something."

· CHAPTER 27 ·

Brainstorming

WHEN THE SECRET COOKING CLUB gathers in the living room of Violet's aunt's house, everyone starts talking at once. "Who used the stove last?" Gretchen tries to get to the bottom of things.

"I don't know," Violet says. "Maybe me, or Alison, I don't remember—"

"I'm sure I checked," Alison wails. "It wasn't me."

"Look." I hold up my hand. "This won't help. We're a club, so in some ways we're all responsible." I swallow hard. "Besides, I went into the kitchen last—"

"You're right. It doesn't matter," Gretchen says. "It happened, and we need to move on—together."

Everyone nods glumly. I pass around a bowl of tasteless cheese crackers.

"We could meet here sometimes," Violet volunteers. "As long as we clean up really well. Aunt Hilda doesn't cook, and she doesn't like the smell of food in the kitchen."

"What good is a kitchen where you can't cook?" Gretchen says disdainfully.

"We could meet at my house," Alison says. "Mom doesn't get home from work until seven. She doesn't cook either, but she's got a lot of stuff we could use."

I shake my head. "That's not the point. Even if we could find somewhere else, it won't be the same."

"I agree," Violet says. "Besides, we've made things worse for Mrs. Simpson; her nephew's threatening to send her to an old people's home because she can't look after herself. We can't just leave her to be locked away eating mushy food until she dies."

"Mushy food?" Alison looks horrified. "She'd hate that."

I clear my throat to get things back on track. "And anyway," I say, "she's teaching us. I've never had a mentor before."

"Me neither," Gretchen says. "And I guess she must have enjoyed it too if she wants us to come back. So, what do we do?"

"Well, I was kind of hoping you might have some ideas," I say. "Since you're involved in the PTA and all that."

Gretchen gives me an exasperated look. "Have you ever been to a PTA meeting?"

"No."

She shakes her head. "Forget it."

"I have an idea." Alison flicks a lock of blond hair out of her eyes. The three of us turn toward her. I stifle a mean thought that it's probably the first time she's ever spoken those words. "Well, I *do*." Alison glares at Gretchen (who must have been thinking the same as me). "I was thinking maybe we could have a bake-a-thon or something."

I sit back in my chair. "Go on…"

"I don't know. Maybe we could get sponsors and advertisers, and people could make pledges to a PayPal account. Nick says you can raise money by doing stuff online. I mean…look at your mom." She glances sideways at me like she's still trying to figure out why I deserve to have a "celebrity" in the family.

The mention of Nick Farr makes my cheeks go hot. "Well, I don't know anything about what Mom does, other than make my life miserable," I say. "Besides, even if we raised money, what good would that do?"

"Mrs. Simpson could hire a nurse or caregiver," Gretchen says. "That's what happened when my grandma got really old.

The caregiver came in once a day at first. At the end, she was there around the clock."

"It's definitely something to consider, I guess."

"But what about Mr. Kruffs?" Violet says. She lowers her voice. "Aunt Hilda said he's eager to have Mrs. Simpson sell her house. I think he owns a share of it or something. Maybe that's why he's trying to get rid of her."

"That's pretty low," Gretchen says.

"You know," I say, "there is one thing that we might be able to do about Mr. Kruffs if he causes trouble."

"What's that?" Violet asks.

"Well…" I think out loud. "I know how stressed my mom gets over her 'online image' and the number of Facebook friends and Twitter followers she has. She's always going on about it."

"She's got tons, hasn't she?" Gretchen says admiringly.

"But she's always trying to get more. And if Mr. Kruffs is running for office, he's probably worried about his public image too."

"The senior vote!" Gretchen says. "That's what you call it when you want old people to vote for you."

"Yeah. And it wouldn't look very good if everyone knew he put his aunt in a home, would it?"

"No!" Violet's eyes blaze. "I wouldn't vote for him. No way."

"So, if he tries anything, we expose him."

"Okay," Gretchen says. "It's a start. And now, we'd better head over to her house."

"Yeah." Alison stands quickly. "I'm starving, and I want to cook something, not sit around here." She eyes the bowl of crackers disdainfully.

"Me too." I stand while Violet tosses the rest of the crackers in the trash. "Let's go."

We go to Mrs. Simpson's house and ring the doorbell. There's no outward sign there ever was a fire, or that anyone is home. Or whether or not Mr. Kruffs came over as promised. After a minute there's no answer, so I knock hard on the door. A wave of anxiety rises inside me.

"Is the key still there?" Violet says. "We ought to at least check that she's okay."

I bend down and look under the mat. The key is there as usual. I unlock the door, and we all go inside. There's a smell of smoke, and the house is quiet as though it's holding its breath. I tiptoe toward the light under the kitchen door, feeling nervous.

As I'm about to turn the knob, a voice comes from inside. "You're two minutes late."

Mrs. Simpson's voice.

I open the door. Part of the wall is charred black, the window is covered with cardboard, and there are towels mopping up the last of the water on the floor. Mrs. Simpson's copper kettle is on the stove with steam coming out of it—at least the stove seems to be working. I suck in a breath through my teeth, feeling guilty all over again.

Mrs. Simpson looks up from where she's sitting at the table, cookbooks spread out in front of her. There's also a piece of paper and a pen.

"I'm sorry we're late," I say. "And just so you know, we all wanted to say—"

She holds up her hand to silence me.

"You wanted to say you're sorry, and that it won't happen again. I know all that, so let's skip it and get down to business." She lifts her chin proudly.

"Yes, Mrs. Simpson," we all say in unison.

"I've made up a menu." She holds up the piece of paper. "Four of you, and four courses. Sound fair enough?"

OMG!

For the next few hours, I forget about the fire, my problems, Mrs. Simpson's problems, and everything else—except trying to cook something special that meets her high standards.

CHAPTER 28

An Idea

AT SCHOOL THE NEXT DAY I daydream about the evening at Mrs. Simpson's house. For the first time ever, I ate like I was in a five-star restaurant. There was French onion soup with homegrown herbs, spicy crab cakes with dill mayonnaise, perfectly marinated rib-eye steaks with tender vegetables, and for dessert, my own special creation—a mint and strawberry chocolate soufflé.

Mrs. Simpson didn't even lift a spoon during the cooking process, but she hovered over each step, approving the measuring and mixing of ingredients as if she was four people at once. She also set the table with fine, gold-rimmed china, snow-white linen place mats and napkins, and gold and silver candles. We didn't talk about the fire, or her worries, or any of our own.

Once, as we were cooking, I'd tried to ask her about the

little recipe book hoping she'd tell us more about the dedica-
tion: *To my little cook— May you find the secret ingredient.*
"It's a really lovely little book," I'd said. "It must have taken
you a long time to make."

But Mrs. Simpson didn't answer right away. Her breathing seemed to grow shallow, and I could tell I'd upset her. But
a moment later, she'd recovered. "It was a long time ago," she'd
said, her hand trembling as she raised a teacup to her lips. I'd
taken the hint—and Violet had helpfully changed the subject
by asking a question about how long to cook the vegetables.

When dinner was served, Mrs. Simpson got each of us to
talk about ourselves: our happiest times, our best memories,
what we want to be when we grow up—stuff that might seem
silly, but actually was nice to share.

Gretchen talked a lot about her family and how close they
are. I already knew her dad is a lawyer, but I didn't know her
mom is the head of HR for some bank. Or that she has an
older brother who works for a clean water charity in Africa. No
wonder Gretchen tries hard to be Ms. Perfect. And succeeds—
most of the time, at least. "I want to study law like my dad," she
said proudly. "So I can help people with their problems. But
I'll need to know how to cook for when I'm at college. And,
you know, after."

Alison acted unusually shy when Mrs. Simpson asked her about her future ambitions. Before answering, she looked at Gretchen as if seeking permission. "I wanted to go to ballet school," she told us, "but I had to have an operation on my knee. So, that's not going to be possible now."

I saw her through new eyes, feeling surprised and sympathetic. Alison has turned out to be nicer than I expected, but I didn't know she'd had that happen to her.

"But I'm kind of okay with it," she continued. "I was thinking I could start a dance studio someday. I like working with kids. But who knows…" She smiled in my direction. "Maybe I'll teach cooking too, so that girls who want to be dancers can still eat healthily. It's really fun—I never would have guessed."

Mrs. Simpson nodded thoughtfully. "The best way to eat healthily is to use healthy ingredients—vegetables, nuts, fruits, fish—all as fresh as possible. I've got some special recipes I can show you."

"Great," Alison said. "I'd like that."

When Mrs. Simpson turned to Violet and asked her what she wanted to be, Violet surprised everyone except me by saying she wants to be a doctor. "I want to save lives," she said. Her eyes flicked over to me, but she didn't tell the rest of them what she had told me. "But until I can do that, I'm happy enough baking things. I was really scared to come to a new school," she admitted. "But now that we've got the Secret Cooking Club, I'm glad I did."

"Yeah," I said. "The Secret Cooking Club has been good for all of us."

"And what about you, Scarlett?" Mrs. Simpson asked.

I'd been waiting for the question and made up all kinds of answers in my mind: like winning *Cake Wars*, writing my own cookbook, or helping end world hunger. But instead, I decided to answer truthfully.

"I don't know, really," I said. "I'm kind of just trying to enjoy what I've got now—like you guys."

"Let's toast the Secret Cooking Club," Violet replied, raising her glass.

"To Mrs. Simpson," I said.

"To mixing friends and flour," Gretchen added.

"To buttercream." Alison laughed.

Mrs. Simpson leaned forward. "To friendship," she said.

"Hear, hear."

The kitchen echoed with the tinkling of crystal as we all clinked our glasses together. And even though it took a long time to wash and put away all that fine china, it was a really good night.

But now…

"Hey, Scarlett, wait up!"

I turn around and see the person trying to get my attention is Nick Farr. I feel as if everything I ate for breakfast might come up again. Alison and Gretchen are good friends with Nick, so why does talking to a boy make me so nervous?

"Oh, hi." I stop walking and turn.

"Alison said you needed some help—with an online profile or something?"

"Um, I do—?"

"That's what she said." His cute-as-a-boy-band-member face slips into a frown.

Get a grip, Scarlett! "I mean, yes, I do."

He raises an eyebrow. "I've got my laptop in my bag. I can meet you in the library after school. But I don't have long. I'm helping coach a junior soccer team later tonight."

"Oh."

"Okay, well…" He gives me a look like he's sorry he bothered to speak to me in the first place. "I'll see you later then?"

"Yeah. Thanks."

I make a run for the girls' bathroom. My insides feel liquid and gushy. *Nick Farr spoke to me. Nick Farr is going to meet me after school. OMG! I am going to die/be sick/fall down on my knees and thank Alison/kill Alison/run screaming from the building/go home and change my clothes/wash my hair/take a cold shower/ crawl under the duvet and never come out.*

"So did Nick talk to you?" Violet emerges from the far stall, smiling mischievously.

"You're in on it too! I thought I was going to die."

"Come on, Scarlett." She laughs. "This is your big chance."

"For what?"

She cocks her head like I'm stupid or something. "We all agreed, I thought. If we're online, we might be able to raise money to help Mrs. Simpson."

"But I'm still not sure how." I stare at her without seeing. "Besides, I don't have a clue how to get started."

"Maybe not, but that's where Nick comes in. We all think you'll be a natural—with your mom and stuff—"

"My mom!"

She winks at me and heads to the door. "Let me know how it goes."

The door swooshes shut behind her.

My big chance. I sit in class giving myself a pep talk. Part of me feels betrayed and ganged up on by my friends, but another part feels all giddy and stupidly excited. When school's over for the day, I mostly feel self-conscious and scared. But the main thing I need to focus on is helping Mrs. Simpson stay in her own home.

I put on lip gloss, brush my hair, and go to the school library. I'm half expecting the other members of the Secret Cooking Club to be sitting at a nearby table, giggling and laughing. But other than a couple of kids studying for their exams, the library's empty.

I grab a book from a random shelf and flip halfway through it before I realize it's about the history of train travel in Britain. I slam it shut and put it back. Then I have an idea. I ask the librarian if there's a cooking section. She raises an eyebrow like I've asked for something strange and points me to a shelf at the back.

There are a couple of books for little kids—teddy bear picnics and cooking around the world, plus a few of the usual Alice Waters and Rachael Rays. At the end of the shelf there's a tattered old book bound in blue leather that's turned around back to front. I take it off the shelf. It's a copy of *Recipes Passed Down from Mother to Daughter* that Mrs. Simpson has in her kitchen. I flip through the recipes, realizing that, because of Mrs. Simpson's handmade, handwritten recipe book, I could now cook any of them. Best of all, I'd no longer be scared to try. In fact, I *want* to try them all and share Mrs. Simpson's recipes with even more kids.

And that's exactly what I'm going to do.

CHAPTER 29

The Plan in Action

I'M GOING TO START MY own blog. It's going to be called *The Secret Cooking Club*. I'll put on lots of recipes and photos and inspire other kids to make things especially for their school. There will be posts called "Yummy Cakes and Bakes," one called "Home-Cooked Dinners," and one called "Recipes for Sharing." And then I'll write about this really cool old woman who's helping us and about her special handwritten-recipe book. I'll post photos of the book, the recipes, and all the little drawings and rhymes.

And when it's all up and running, I'll send the link to Mr. Kruffs. He'll see we're online, and if he tries to put Mrs. Simpson in a home, he'll have nothing but bad publicity.

"Hi, Scarlett."

The dream dissolves like sugar in water.

"Oh, um…hi, Nick."

"Sorry I'm late." He plonks his bag down on the table. "I've got to leave in thirty, so let's get started."

"Great." I walk over to the table and sit beside him. I let a curtain of hair fall over my eyes so I can watch his every move. His hands are slender, his fingers graceful as he takes his laptop out of his bag and turns it on.

"So, were you thinking of a blog, or what?" he asks me.

"Yeah, a blog where I can post some photos and people can leave comments," I brainstorm out loud. "Maybe a place for guest posts too."

"So, kind of like your mom's?"

I shudder. I can't believe I'm doing this. "Well, it won't *really* be like hers."

"No, I guess not."

My mind races to think of something to say as the computer boots up.

"My mom won't let me use the internet at home," I ramble. "So I don't really know much about how to build and design blogs. But I thought I might like to learn."

He turns to me. "Are you trying to get back at her?"

"What do you mean?"

"Your mom," he says. "To be honest, I was kind of

surprised when Ali told me you wanted to set up a blog. I've always thought you had it pretty rough, with your mom writing about you and everything."

"You did?" My awkwardness begins to melt away.

"I remember a few years back—you used to always speak up in class. You knew all the answers and you had lots of ideas… You were really smart."

I give him a wobbly smile. "Really?"

"But then you stopped. After people found out about the blog."

"Well, I guess…" I sigh. "Yeah, that's probably true."

He types in his password. "I'm sure your mom is cool and all, but I know I'd hate it if anyone wrote like that about me on the internet."

"She isn't cool. I hate that she does it. Most people don't understand."

He smiles. "Maybe more people understand than you think."

I mull this over as he opens a web page.

"So there are some pretty good blogging sites out there. I think this one's the best." He types something into the browser. "It's pretty easy to post photos, text, and video. And you can search by hashtags—so you can follow people, and people can find you."

"Um…okay."

"Here, I'll show you."

For the next twenty minutes, I half watch what Nick does and half understand it. The rest of the time I'm watching him and enjoying sitting next to the coolest boy in our class who thinks I must be smart, and who "understands" I haven't had things exactly easy. I ask a few questions, but I can't bring myself to ask the BIG question—he and Alison hang out at school and she talks about him all the time—do they have a thing going? Or is there hope for someone like me?

"Scarlett?" I realize Nick is waiting for a response from me.

"Oh, sorry. I was just trying to concentrate—it's a lot to take in."

"Well, I'm sorry I have to take off. But let me know how it's going and if you need any more help." He shuts down his computer.

"Thank you so much," I say. The words can't express my mixed-up feelings. "I know you're busy, but I really appreciate your help."

He hesitates for a second. "Well, if you really want to thank me, there's something you can do for me too."

"Oh, what's that?"

"Would you consider adding a new member?"

CHAPTER 30

The First Post

I'M FULLY PREPARED FOR MY feet not to touch the ground. But actually, I'm remarkably calm as I leave the library. It's like the whole Nick Farr thing has made me grow up all in the course of a single day. I grip the paper with his phone number in my hand. I've agreed to contact him the next time the Secret Cooking Club meets so he can join us!

"For the record, Alison didn't tell me you were the ones leaving the free samples," he'd reassured me after seeing my astonished face. "I guessed that day I saw you out of class just before lunch. And I think it would be fun to learn a little about cooking. I mean, lots of guys do it these days. And Mom and Dad don't have time to cook. It would be nice if I could surprise them by cooking something good once in a while."

"Yeah," I'd said. "I think it's something that anyone can enjoy doing. I mean, we all have to eat, don't we?"

He laughed. "Yes, we do. Also, my mom has a big birthday coming up. Dad's planning a party for her, and I'm supposed to order a cake. But how awesome would it be if I could actually make her one?"

"It sounds great," I said. "And we'd all be happy to pitch in."

"Okay," he said. "My soccer schedule's a little hectic right now, but I should be able to meet you one night next week? Monday?"

He'd written down his number and left for his practice. I'd rushed off to meet the other members at Mrs. Simpson's house.

When I get there and let myself inside, everything is quiet, dark, and empty. In the kitchen, I see that some work has been done to repaint the wall and fix the window. It looks as good as new. Obviously, Mr. Kruffs didn't waste any time getting workmen in. And if he was here, then where is his aunt now? I'm sure we'd arranged to meet her today. I was hoping she would be here so I could tell her about the blog—and about Nick wanting to join us.

I don't feel like going home, so I nose around a little.

Something is scribbled on the magnetic message pad that hangs on the fridge: "Gone to visit a friend—RS."

That explains where Mrs. Simpson is, at least. It must have been a last-minute thing. Relieved, I sit at the table and take a notebook and pen out of my backpack. The words pop into my head and I begin to write:

> Please don't tell my mom you're reading this. I mean, you probably won't because you don't know who I am, so you don't know who she is. And I don't know who you are. For now, I think we ought to keep it that way. It will be our secret.
>
> You see, I have this problem with my mom. She's a blogger, and she's made my life a nightmare by posting lots of embarrassing stuff about me. I pretty much had to drop all my activities at school, it was getting so annoying.

I pause and read over what I've written, crossing out and changing a few words here and there.

> But now I've started doing something Mom doesn't know about. Don't worry, it's nothing

bad. It's just that my neighbor was taken away in an ambulance, and when I went to feed her cat, I found this amazing kitchen and a special handwritten recipe book. And there was this new girl at school, and I told her about what I found, and she wanted to join me. So that's our secret: we're learning how to cook. Now there's five of us—four girls and one boy, plus the old woman whose kitchen we use. We're a real club—a secret club. No one knows who we are.

Except you...

And that's what this blog is about. We'd like you to join us. Leave a comment below, and welcome to the Secret Cooking Club.

> Yours truly,
> The Little Cook
> P.S. Don't tell any grown-ups!

I put down the pen. Luckily, I've read enough of Mom's blog to know how to do it. I think it sounds chatty, and it says what I want to say. I've chosen to sign it as "The Little Cook" in honor of Mrs. Simpson's book. A strange feeling comes over me—not the calm of earlier, but more like the jolt of an electric shock. I was *meant* to come here and find the special recipe book. I'm *meant* to be doing this.

Just then, the front door opens. I jump up and pack my papers away. There's a loud screech and the sound of small feet running. Then, voices:

"Ow, he scratched me!"

"Well, I guess he's just hungry and glad to be home."

"*Achoo!* I'm allergic to fur."

Something small and black darts across the kitchen floor in front of me. "Treacle!" I say happily. The cat goes next to the fridge where his bowl used to be and begins to meow indignantly.

"Hi, Scarlett." Violet comes in with Treacle's bowl in her hand. She puts a finger to her lips. "We were out kidnapping Treacle."

"Kidnapping?"

"Well, cat-napping actually." Gretchen giggles. Alison gives another big sneeze.

"Where was he?" I ask.

"At the cat kennel on Priory Road." Violet sets down his bowl, and I fill it with cat food. "I asked my aunt to find out from Mr. Kruffs where he had taken the cat. She told him we were thinking of adopting him, but really we just wanted to surprise Mrs. Simpson. Do you know where Mrs. Simpson is?"

"She left a note—she's visiting a friend."

"Oh," Violet says. "That's good, I guess. We came here earlier. The workmen were just leaving, but I was a little worried when she wasn't here."

"Let's try to cook something, and maybe she'll be back in time for supper."

The four of us start raiding the fridge and cupboards. Violet suggests we try to make Simple Simon's Cottage Pie.

I fetch the minced beef while Gretchen and Alison go out to the garden to pick some of the end-of-season vegetables. Violet chops the potatoes before mashing them.

"Where were you, by the way?" Violet says. Her little smirk tells me she knows exactly where I was.

My calm, cool resolve fades, and I break out into a silly grin. It's all just too insane to think I was setting up a blog with Nick Farr, and that he wants to join us. Gretchen and Alison come back inside. I suddenly feel self-conscious.

"So how did your meeting go?" Alison says, her eyes watering from the cat.

"Um, good, I think."

"You think?" Gretchen jeers. "Come on, Scarlett. You can do better than that."

"Well, he's going to help me set up a blog. An online Secret Cooking Club—I thought we'd have different posts like 'Yummy Cakes and Bakes,' 'Home-Cooked Dinners,' and 'Recipes for Sharing.'"

"What about something healthy too?" Alison suggests. "Like 'Healthy Bites for Home'? Mrs. Simpson showed me a great recipe for fruit-and-nut protein bars. I'm dying to try them."

"I like it!" I grin at Alison.

"Okay, okay," Violet says. "Now stop avoiding the real subject. How was it meeting...*him*?" she coaxes.

My face flushes. "It was fine. Actually, Nick wants to join us."

"Join us?" Gretchen and Violet say at the same time.

Alison shrugs. "I guess he keeps things buttoned up. He didn't say anything to me."

"It will be really cool to have a boy member," Violet says.

"Especially Nick Farr, right, Scarlett?" Gretchen winks at me and blows a kiss.

"Very funny," I sulk. *Is it that obvious Nick makes me feel so strange—bubbly one minute and self-conscious the next?* "But the more the merrier."

"Maybe he'll invite the rest of the soccer team," Violet says. "They must eat a lot."

"Maybe," I say. "But first we need to focus on helping Mrs. Simpson. Here's what I have in mind..."

I outline my idea to the group. How we'll start a blog, get lots of followers and friends, and raise money to help Mrs. Simpson and other elderly people living alone.

"It might work." Gretchen says. "I mean, look at all the sponsors your mom has."

"And like Alison suggested, we can have a bake-a-thon. But we'll do it online. We'll get sponsors and advertisers and pledges. And if we can get other kids to join us—kids from all over the place—they can bake things too."

Alison beams. The bake-a-thon was her idea, after all. But it's Gretchen who takes up the brainstorming. "It's a really good idea, Scarlett," she says. "And once we've got an online profile, if Mr. Kruffs tries to force his aunt out of her home, we'll tell all his voters."

"Do you really think it might work?" Violet says.

"Well, unless anyone has any better ideas," Gretchen says, "let's give it a try."

"Okay, we will. And, there's just one other thing..." Taking a deep breath, I turn back to Alison. I can't believe the words are coming out of my mouth. "I was wondering about Nick. Is he…um…your—"

Gretchen and Violet look at each other and laugh. Alison's perfect skin flushes a lovely shade of peach.

"No, silly," Alison says. "He's my cousin."

CHAPTER 31

Mom's Little Helper

MY MIND BUBBLES LIKE A boiling pot. The new blog, Mr. Kruffs, Mrs. Simpson—where is she anyway?—and the most distracting of all, the fact that Alison is *not* going out with Nick Farr. He's her cousin! No wonder she's so relaxed around him.

We finish making the pies—they have fluffy mashed potato tops that are just browned, and the meat filling has lots of fresh vegetables, gravy, and herbs in it. In the end, they are simple, but delicious. But for once, I can't finish mine. I pack the rest of it up in a plastic container, along with the one we made for Mrs. Simpson. Despite the note she left, it's getting late and I'm starting to get worried.

We all pitch in to do the cleaning up (double- and triple-checking the oven and stove are turned off). Treacle curls up in his basket next to the oven. I stay behind after the others have left, hoping Mrs. Simpson might return. She doesn't. Eventually, I decide to go home. I lock the door and put the key back under the mat.

At home, I'm surprised to hear the TV on. It's way past Kelsie's bedtime, and Mom is always too busy to watch anything. But when I go into the living room, I see her—sprawled out on the sofa, asleep, her laptop half falling off her lap. At first I worry she tried to wait up for me (luckily, both of us seem to have forgotten that, technically, I'm supposed to be grounded). Then I realize she's just exhausted. For a second, I feel sorry for her.

I turn off the TV and watch her sleep for a minute, my brain pondering an idea. She won't allow me internet access at home, so I won't be able to upload my post or update my new blog. But maybe there's something I can do to change that.

I move the laptop off her legs, and she jerks awake. "Scarlett?" She looks around her as if she's in a strange place. Then she sees the laptop in my hand and reaches for it. "Thanks for waking me," she says. "I've got some things to finish."

"That's okay, Mom. I'm sorry you're so tired."

"Well..." She shrugs. "I guess that goes with the territory."

"I was thinking...maybe I could help you. With some of

your blog stuff. I could answer emails and post updates, maybe even respond to comments if you showed me how."

Mom gives me a suspicious frown. "You've never shown an interest before."

"Well, we're learning about computer stuff at school. So I could use some practice."

"Is this a new club you've joined?"

"No," I say quickly. "It's just that everyone else knows how to use computers and social media. I should learn it too."

"You're probably right." She purses her lips in thought. "Social media is important. I guess maybe you are old enough to use it responsibly. But we'd need to set strict controls." I can sense her blog-cogs whirring: "Help! My Daughter Wants To Be Online. Is This Payback?" For once, I don't let it bother me.

"Of course, Mom," I concede. "And if I helped you, then you wouldn't have to work so hard all the time."

"Hmm. I'll think about it."

"I...um, could start now?"

"I'm too tired to show you right now."

"Okay, but once I've had a little practice, I'll be able to do a bunch. You'll need all your energy for your launch in Superdrug."

"Well...I'll sleep on it." She closes the laptop and sets it on the coffee table. Her mouth opens into a big yawn. "Don't stay up too late."

"Okay, I won't."

I haven't exactly gotten permission, but Mom's not one to turn down an offer of free help—even from me. We both go upstairs, and as soon as I hear her bedroom door shut and the water running in the bathtub, I creep back downstairs. I go to the living room and open her laptop. It turns on immediately, but it asks for a password.

Determined not to fall at the first hurdle, I go into the kitchen and try the door to the Mom Cave. It doesn't open. I push harder, thinking the door must be stuck, but it still doesn't open. It must be locked. I've never known Mom to lock it before.

I try the kitchen junk drawer to see if there's a spare key. As I'm digging through the pieces of paper, old bills, and yellow sticky notes, there's a loud thump from behind the door to the Mom Cave. I go back over and put my ear to the door. Everything is quiet—I must have imagined it.

I look again for a key, but find instead a yellow sticky with the name and number of a computer repairman. On the back,

Mom's scribbled her password: scarlettkelsie1. I'm surprised and even a little bit touched that she's used our names as her password. I return to the computer and type it in. The screen flickers to life.

Okay, I'm in…now what? I pull up the blog website. From there, it takes me a confusing and slightly nerve-racking half hour to set up an account. I have to sign up for an email account on another site, verify my address, choose my template, and figure out how to move around text boxes and photo layouts. Finally, I open a new text box, and slowly and carefully so I don't make too many mistakes, I type in my first blog post as the "Little Cook."

When I'm finished typing, I look over what I've done. It's fine—I guess—but on the screen, it seems kind of dull and boring. I realize almost immediately what's missing. Mom always uses lots of cringeworthy pictures in her blog—irritating 1950s moms in aprons vacuuming or doing laundry—with little sayings like "If only you'd do what I say, Mommy wouldn't have to LOSE HER MIND" or making up not-so-funny award badges for things like "Today I Survived Washing My Daughter's Gym Clothes." All of her friends and followers always comment on how good they are. For my blog, I need some pictures too. Gretchen and Alison have both taken photos with their phones of some of the things we've made. That should work for a start.

I spend the next half hour trying to add some empty boxes with the cursor where the photos will eventually go. But everything I've written ends up on the wrong lines or disappearing half off the page. Frustrated, I save what I've done as a draft and shut it down before I can make it any worse.

I'll just have to ask Nick. Poor me!

CHAPTER 32

An Unwanted Visitor

BEFORE I LEAVE FOR SCHOOL the next morning I go over to Mrs. Simpson's house. Treacle is inside, meowing at the door, and there's no sign Mrs. Simpson has been home. My stomach knots with worry. Maybe she came home and Mr. Kruffs had her old-lady-napped. Or maybe she tried to get somewhere on her own and was hurt or injured. When we're cooking with her, she doesn't seem old and frail at all. But I remember the other times: in the hospital and the night of the fire...

Violet sees my face when I meet up with her in the hallway. Her smile fades to worry. "She's not back yet?"

"No. What can we do?"

"I don't know. Are you free after school?"

"Um, yeah." I hesitate. "But I've got a couple of questions for Nick—about the blog."

Her eyes light up in amusement. "I bet you do."

I give her a nasty look and walk off to class.

It takes me the whole morning to psych myself up to talk to Nick at lunchtime in the cafeteria. He's talking with one of his soccer friends, but looks up as I come over to his table. I shift awkwardly from foot to foot.

"Hi," I say, my voice croaky. "Thanks for your help yesterday. I've, uh…got a few follow-up questions."

His friend raises an eyebrow across the table.

"Yeah, whatever." Nick shrugs. I'm immediately sorry I came up to him in front of his friend. "I can't do it today—maybe tomorrow?"

"Tomorrow?" I repeat dumbly. "Yeah, that would be great."

Before I can embarrass myself any further, I quickly turn and make a beeline for the girls' bathroom. I practically slam into Gretchen and Alison, who are standing at the sink painting their nails with rainbow stripes of pink and purple polish.

Gretchen gives me a disdainful look for the benefit of another girl who's at the sink washing her hands. As soon as the girl leaves, Gretchen shrugs apologetically. "Hi, Scarlett," she says. "What's up?"

"I need your photos for the blog," I say. "All the stuff we've cooked."

"I can upload the photos and help out with the website if you want," Alison offers. "You're going to need some help." She gives a little smirk. "Unless you and Nick want to do it all yourselves."

"No," I say. I see in the mirror that I'm blushing. "I can definitely use some help. Besides," I lower my voice, "we also need to find Mrs. Simpson."

"What?" Gretchen says, looking concerned.

"She's not back yet," I say.

"And you have no idea where she is or who this 'friend' is she went to visit?"

"None at all. It's like she's vanished."

We agree to meet at Mrs. Simpson's house after school as usual. But everyone seems a little preoccupied. It's not as though Mrs. Simpson was around at the start, but already she's become just as important as any of the other members. *More* important, considering she's teaching us, and we're using her kitchen and special recipe book.

The house is still empty when we get there. Treacle meows

plaintively like he's lonely—and maybe a little unhappy with us for rescuing him. Which he probably is. We find a recipe that we all agree on: Peter Piper's Pepper Pasta. Gretchen and Alison go out to the garden to pick tomatoes while Violet and I mix up the fresh pasta dough. But my heart isn't in it. It takes forever before the pasta is ready to use: We have to roll the dough and cut the pasta, draping long strands around the kitchen. Gretchen and Alison have made a big bowl of salad and started stirring the spices into the sauce. It all smells delicious, and my stomach is growling. Now, if only Mrs. Simpson would come back—

All of a sudden, there's a loud knocking on the front door.

"Aunt Rosemary! Open up!" a voice calls out.

The four of us freeze, looking at each other in horror. It's Mr. Kruffs. We've been caught red-handed!

"Aunt Rosemary, you know we need to talk. You're only making things worse for yourself by not answering my calls. I'm coming in."

A key rattles in the lock. The door bangs open. Instantly, I'm roused into action.

I head him off at the kitchen door. "Hello, Mr. Kruffs," I say, faking a pleasant smile. Violet comes up silently beside me.

"Where is she?" he says accusingly.

"She?" I give Violet a puzzled look. "I thought the cat was a boy cat, didn't you?"

Violet giggles. "I never looked."

"Not the cat!" Mr. Kruffs snaps. "I'm looking for my aunt."

"Oh." I shrug dramatically. "Sorry, haven't seen her today. She left a note—she's visiting a friend."

"Friend? What friend?"

"She didn't say."

He crosses his arms. "And what, may I ask, are you doing here if she's not in?"

"Like I said the last time, I'm Mrs. Simpson's neighbor," I say. "And her friend. We all are." I'm relieved when Gretchen and Alison come up to the door behind me. Now it's four against one.

"You shouldn't be here," he says. "You're trespassing."

I put my hands on my hips, feeling suddenly brave. "So, call the police. They might find it interesting that *you're* bullying an old woman—taking her cat away from her and trying to force her out of her own home. And even if they don't want to listen to us, I'm sure your voters might."

Mr. Kruffs takes a step forward. I grip Violet's hand and stand my ground. OMG.

"You don't know what you're talking about," he says. "My

aunt can't keep living here on her own. It's my responsibility to make arrangements for her."

"What, so that you can sell her house and get the money for your campaign—is that it?" Violet says. I squeeze her hand gratefully.

He actually looks puzzled for a second, and then starts to laugh. "Is that what you think? That's the most ridiculous thing I've ever heard."

"Well, I don't know."

"No, you don't," he says firmly. "And we're done with this conversation. Go home."

"Okay, girls," Gretchen says breezily. "You heard the man. Let's go."

"But what about the—"

Gretchen cuts me off with a raised hand. "We'll just have to leave Mr. Kruffs to do the cleaning up." Gretchen turns back to him. "We were cooking supper. The kitchen's kind of a mess." She smiles wryly. "Could you make sure the oven and burners are turned off when you go?"

"You were using the kitchen?"

"Of course," I answer. "Your aunt is teaching us how to cook. She's not here right now, but we have to practice. We can't let her down."

"She's teaching you to cook—" He stops abruptly, looking genuinely startled.

"Yeah," Alison chimes in. "She's a great teacher—the best. And she knows so much about cooking—she even wrote a special recipe book that we're using. The only thing wrong with her is that she's a little old, that's all."

"Rosemary hasn't cooked in years. Not since Marianne died."

"Marianne?" I say.

"Her daughter. But since you're such good 'friends,' I would have thought you knew that."

To my little cook— May you find the secret ingredient. I swallow a lump in my throat. Mrs. Simpson wrote the special recipe book for her daughter, Marianne. A daughter who died.

Mr. Kruffs raises his hands in a gesture of futility. "Aunt Rosemary heats up canned soup and barely eats that. A year ago she lost so much weight that she was wasting away. She had to be put on electrolytes and fiber." He looks at me pointedly, like I should know what that is.

"Sounds awful," I mutter.

"Yes," he says. "Not eating properly is one of the reasons she can't stay here by herself."

"But her fridge is always full of food," I protest. "She

has an amazing kitchen and all these cookbooks. She *wrote* a cookbook by hand for her daughter. It's obviously her passion."

Mr. Kruffs laughs gruffly. "And do you really think my aunt goes out to the stores and brings all the food back herself? Or do you believe there's a baking fairy that crawls out of her special cookbook at night and hides out in one of the cupboards?"

"No, of course not." I don't tell him that actually, we've all wondered why the kitchen is always well-stocked with food.

"Well, think about it. She doesn't drive, and the supermarket is too far away for her to walk there."

"So?"

"So I have food delivered to her, or, at least, my personal assistant takes care of it. Every week, like clockwork. And not just from the local supermarket, since I know how my aunt appreciates real food. It's from a gourmet market—they even put everything in the cupboards where it belongs, or out on the counter, in case it might encourage her to try cooking something again. It's not cheap, believe me. But I don't want my aunt to starve, now do I?"

"No..." I admit, as I'm struck by a new possibility. What if Mr. Kruffs is genuinely concerned for his aunt? We've only been cooking with her for a short time—surely he must know lots of things we don't. What if before we met her she wasn't eating? And she did have a fall that put her in the hospital…

"And now she's gone missing, and you're here. She doesn't have any friends anymore that live close by. So where is she?"

"I don't know," I concede. "And I can see why you're concerned." I look at my friends. Everyone nods worriedly. "But honestly, your aunt seems okay. When we've been around her, she's seemed happy, and she's eaten the stuff we've cooked for her. So maybe she's doing better than you think?"

He gives me a long look, and I can feel sweat beading up on my forehead. I raise my chin and try to sound like a grown-up. "Mr. Kruffs, would you like to stay a little longer and have some of the supper we've been cooking? It's just salad and pasta with homemade sauce—the recipe is from your aunt's special book." I think of what Mom would say in her blog and take a deep breath. "It might be a good idea if we all sit and talk."

CHAPTER 33

The Warning

HE STARES AT ME. I stare back. The others look at me—surprise and shock on their faces. My heart bangs inside my chest.

"Okay," he says. "Let's talk."

What have I done?

Violet and Alison practically flatten each other in their hurry to set an extra place at the table. I'm amazingly relieved when Gretchen gestures for our guest to take a chair and sits opposite him. She sits up tall, looking every inch the cool, calm, collected PTA rep and future lawyer that all the grown-ups love.

Mr. Kruffs crosses his arms, looking for a moment as if he's sorry he accepted the invite. I bring the huge wooden bowl of freshly tossed salad over to the table and sit next to Gretchen.

"So, Mr. Kruffs…" Gretchen says, "how's the campaign going?"

"It's going just fine." His gaze focuses on me.

"That's what my dad says. You may know him— Alan Sandburg."

"He's your father?" Mr. Kruffs straightens up in his chair.

"Yeah." Gretchen smiles smugly. "He says you're a real champion of the senior vote."

"Of course," Mr. Kruffs says. "Our senior citizens are important members of society. We need to respect and value them."

"And I suppose you'll have to travel up to the capital a lot if you're elected."

"That's right. I'll be there most of the time. I've got a trip planned for early next week."

"Don't you have any family here?" I ask. Violet and Alison sit, and I pass Mr. Kruffs the salad bowl.

He serves himself a generous plateful. "I'm divorced," he says. "So, no. Other than Rosemary, of course."

"It's so nice of you to care so much about your aunt," Violet says. It sounds like she means it. I frown.

Mr. Kruffs spoons on some oil-and-vinegar dressing and passes the salad bowl on to Alison. "Whether you believe it or not, I do care about her. As I said, Aunt Rosemary is my only relative. Once, she was almost like a mother to me. But her health has been getting worse lately. She's scattered and forgetful, and sometimes she's unsteady on her feet. Of course, she won't talk about it, but I think she may be suffering from dementia."

"And what is that exactly?" Gretchen says.

"In simple terms, it means she's losing her memory." Mr. Kruffs takes a bite of salad and chews thoughtfully. "It happens to lots of old people. There's no cure, and she'll only get worse and worse. She might forget to turn off the stove, or she might forget to get dressed or feed the cat—or even eat regular meals. She's a danger to herself, and I can't always be around to look in on her—even if she wanted me to."

We all eat our salad in silence. I mull over what he's just said.

"These tomatoes…" Mr. Kruffs muses. "I must say, they do taste very fresh."

"Your aunt grows them in her garden," Violet says. "They're totally organic."

"My aunt *grows* them?"

"Yeah."

He narrows his eyes and finishes off his plate of salad. When he's finished, Alison jumps up and brings over the steaming bowl of spaghetti. It smells delicious, but I know I can't eat another bite. Not until I confess to what happened.

"Mr. Kruffs, there's something you need to know," I say, trying to keep my voice steady. "Your aunt didn't leave the stove on that time it caught fire." I grip the edge of the table. "We did—accidentally. She was teaching us how to cook eggs Benedict from her special recipe book. We forgot to turn off the gas, and it was my fault that the dish towel caught fire. Not hers."

Mr. Kruffs's face twists into a scowl. "What did you say?"

"I said we started that fire, not your aunt."

He sits back, stunned. "I could call the police right now. What you did was dangerous and stupid—not to mention a waste of public resources."

"It was dangerous and stupid," I admit. "But…it was an accident. It won't happen again."

I bite my tongue, waiting for the explosion I'm sure is coming. Will he jump up and push over the table, shattering everything on the floor? Will he really call the police or drag us out himself?

So, I'm surprised when he reaches for the bowl of pasta and serves himself a heaping pile.

"Here's the sauce," Gretchen says. Her hands are shaking as she passes him the bowl.

He dips the ladle in the sauce, holds it up, and looks closely at it. Then he pours it over the pasta. He takes a bite, barely chewing it before diving in to take another. The rest of us watch in stunned silence—in a few seconds, he's demolished half the serving.

He sets down his fork and wipes his mouth with a napkin. "It was brave of you to confess," he says.

My friends and I all breathe at once.

"Not that it changes anything," he says. He passes the bowl to Gretchen, who takes a small portion for herself and hands it to Violet.

"It doesn't?" I croak.

"No."

I swallow hard. "But maybe Mrs. Simpson doesn't really have dementia or whatever. If she's a little scattered sometimes, it might just be because she's old. And maybe she's sad about her daughter too." *My little cook.* Gretchen gives me a sharp jab with her elbow. I ignore it. "When did she die?" I say.

"Two years ago," Mr. Kruffs says. "It was a car accident."

Violet breathes in sharply.

"It was quick and painless—so they say—but she was Rosemary's only child. No parent should have to outlive their child."

"Did Rosemary's daughter like to cook?" I ask.

"Like to?" He nods. "She was amazing. She went to cooking school in Paris and Switzerland, and she became a professional chef in New York. The restaurant where she worked was awarded a Michelin star while she was there. I remember the Christmas dinners they used to cook together—it was like a banquet there was so much food. And all of it was perfect." He smiles faintly. "They were happy times."

"It's just *so* tragic," Alison wails as she spoons sauce on to her pasta.

"Yes," I say. The food comes around to me. "But that doesn't mean Mrs. Simpson has dementia or is losing her memory. Maybe she's just sad—or lonely—or bored. Maybe she needs something else to do."

Mr. Kruffs shakes his head. "As I said, her health is suffering. She needs to be looked after. And I can't do that. There are some very nice places out there with very nice people. Whatever you might have heard"—he snorts, sounding annoyed—"and people say some idiotic things about homes for the elderly…well, there are a lot of good, kind places where older people are very happy. And safe. She'd make new friends too. It's just what she needs."

"But we're her friends," I say, feeling more and more upset. "That's got to count for something"

"'Friends' that practically burned down her house?" He glares at me. "I think she can do without those, don't you?"

"It was an accident!"

"But it happened."

I cross my arms. "I know you're her nephew, but you can't just make her leave her home and go into one of *those* places."

"Actually, I can." His eyes glint coldly. "I have her power of attorney, which means I can make decisions on her behalf. And I own a share of this house."

"But it's cruel! She doesn't want to go—"

Gretchen elbows me even harder this time. I snap my mouth shut and stare sullenly down at my plate.

"I understand what you're saying about your aunt, Mr. Kruffs. Really, I do." Gretchen passes him back the bowl of pasta. "My grandma was in poor health and needed care before she died. A caregiver came to visit her every day. And Dad installed an emergency button in case something happened when the nurse wasn't there."

Mr. Kruffs fills his plate with seconds. "I don't think that's going to be enough. In the last few months, I've become convinced she needs around-the-clock care."

And then you can sell her house? I open my mouth again, but Gretchen cuts me off with a look.

"It's just something to think about." Gretchen sounds like a real adult. "An option."

Mr. Kruffs doesn't answer. He's back to eating the pasta like it's going out of style. I inhale the steam coming from my plate. Now that Gretchen's taken charge, I take a small bite. The fresh herbs and the spices of the sauce tingle on my tongue, the vegetables full of delicious flavor. The homemade pasta is silky and rich.

"This food..." Mr. Kruffs says, wiping his mouth on a napkin, "...is delicious."

"Oh, do you think so?" Violet smiles brightly. "I'm so glad. Your aunt would be proud to hear you say so."

He shakes his head in disbelief.

The bowls of pasta and sauce get passed around again, and the food is gone in a few minutes. "Would you like some dessert?" Gretchen offers him.

"Unfortunately, I'm going to have to pass," Mr. Kruffs says. "I must run. The fact is, my aunt is still missing. I have to phone around and try to find her."

"Has she done it before?" Violet asks.

He pauses before answering. "A few times. Unfortunately, any old friends she has are scattered here and there. She's gone to complete strangers' houses before, looking for people she used to know who died years ago."

"Oh." I don't really have a good answer to that.

"Is it okay if we stay to do the washing up?" Alison asks. "We'll check to make sure everything is turned off and we'll lock up."

"You do that," he says. "But from now on, you need to find somewhere else to do your cooking—do you understand?"

"Yeah," I say. The breath leaves my body like a punctured balloon.

"I'm leaving next week for a day or so," he continues. "Tuesday morning, early. If she's not back home by the weekend, I'm calling the police."

"Fair enough," Gretchen says.

I nod.

"Thanks for eating with us," Violet cheerfully changes the subject. "I think we all understand each other much better now."

"It's been...interesting." Mr. Kruffs runs a hand through his dark hair. He nods curtly at us, then turns and walks out.

As soon as he's gone, the four of us open our mouths as if to talk at once, and yet no one speaks. Violet clears the plates from the table, and Alison runs a sink full of hot soapy water.

"What now?" I find my voice and turn to Gretchen.

"You didn't help things by getting annoyed like that," she scolds.

"And you sure were a Miss Goody-Two-Shoes, sucking up to him like that—"

"I can't believe you told him about the fire!"

"Well, we can't let him keep believing that she did it, can we?"

"Okay, okay," Violet intervenes. "That's enough. We need to think about what we do next."

"We have to hope Mrs. Simpson comes back," Alison says. "If he has to call the police, it will make things a lot worse for her."

"Alison's right," Gretchen says. "There's not much we can do unless we find her."

"But if she does come back, then how do we know we can trust *him*?" I say.

Gretchen smiles cryptically. "Once she's back, I think Mr. Kruffs will come around to our way of thinking."

"What makes you so sure?" I snap. "He seemed like a total creep to me."

Gretchen rolls her eyes. "Honestly, Scarlett. Don't you ever read your mom's blog? She's always saying that the way to a man's heart is through his stomach."

CHAPTER 34

Hiding Out

I'M RELIEVED WHEN I GET home that night: We've stood up to Mr. Kruffs and given him more than just food for thought. Though I have to admit—Gretchen's grown-up way of dealing with him might have been more effective than mine. But there's still one big problem—where's Mrs. Simpson?

For the second night in a row, Mom is working on her laptop in the living room. Her hair is tangled and stringy, and she has dark circles under her eyes. But sitting on the table next to her is a tasty-looking cupcake with pink frosting, and the crumbs and wrapper of one already eaten.

"Hello, Mom," I say, putting down my bag.

"Scarlett." She smiles wearily and checks her watch. "Let me guess—working hard on your science project?"

"Yeah, Mom, it's going to be really cool when we finish."

"I'm glad you've made a new friend. What did you say her name was?"

"Violet."

"Violet. That's pretty—like Scarlett." She smiles.

"Yeah." I start to head off.

"Sometimes I worry that you don't have friends because…" She hesitates. "Well, you know…"

I stop.

"…because of me," she finishes in a whisper.

I stare at her in disbelief. "Because of you?"

"I know, it was a silly thought." She gives a little laugh. "I mean, no one knows who I am for real, or who you are."

"Um…"

"Except the people at Superdrug, of course. And maybe anyone who might recognize my profile picture. So really, I know it's not an issue. But you know…" she says, brightening further, "I've had this idea lately. That I might move in a whole different direction."

I'm not sure I like the sound of that. I press my lips together. Now that I think about it, it's been a few weeks since she's written any bad blog posts about me. After "The Single Mom's Guide to Dating," she wrote a post for another site on "Best Mom-Friendly Day Spas," and this week's Friday post will be "Psst—I'm in Superdrug!" about her upcoming product launch. If that equals a new direction, then maybe I should be all for it.

"But anyway…" She shrugs. "We'll see."

"Sounds…interesting," I manage.

"Would you like a cupcake?" She gestures to the plate. "They're really nice. I had a big dinner and can't eat another bite."

"Oh." I look closely at her. Mom's usual idea of dinner is a little cup of yogurt and a bag of potato chips—maybe a slice of cold pizza now and then. And certainly not cupcakes. I remember what Gretchen said about Mom's blog and the way to a man's heart—maybe she's planning to start dating again. That would probably be a good thing—give her lots of stuff to blog about other than me.

"I'll have it later, Mom," I say. "And if you want to go to bed early, I can help you with your work—like we agreed the other night."

She rummages through her papers. "I've printed out some emails for you to update my contacts. Do you think you can do that?"

"Yeah, I can."

"Well, then…" She stands and flexes her fingers wearily.

"I'll leave you to it. And just remember—I'm trusting you not to be looking at any websites you shouldn't. You know, I can always check."

I give an offended shrug. "Whatever, Mom. I'm just trying to help you. But if you'd rather I didn't—"

"No, Scarlett, I appreciate your help." She walks to the door. "As I said, I trust you."

"Oh, Mom, one more thing."

She turns back toward me. "What?"

"Is something wrong with your office?"

"No," she says a little too quickly. "It's just that I can always smell cooking from the other side of the wall. It's really distracting."

I eat the cupcake and update Mom's contacts. When I'm finished, I log into my blog. I'm not too worried that Mom might actually check up on me. Even if she sees I accessed a cooking blog, what's the harm in that? I click on my draft blog post to update it. I manage to upload the pictures of our food creations that Alison emailed to me. The layout isn't quite right, but I'm satisfied I've done the best I can. I hit the icon to publish my first post as the Little Cook.

The Secret Cooking Club Online is now officially live.

I surf for a while, looking at other cooking blogs. I check back a few times to see if there's any sign that anyone has seen my blog. Of course, no one has—it's only been up for minutes—what am I expecting? But then a little warning flashes on at the bottom of the screen: low battery. Mom doesn't have the power cord in the living room. It must be in the Mom Cave.

I set the laptop aside and go to the kitchen. I'm surprised to see a bunch of pots and pans on the drainer next to the sink, all washed up and drying. Mom wasn't kidding when she said she had a big dinner. There are also three plates. Mom, Kelsie...and...?

As unlikely as it may seem, I *know* who.

I go to the back of the kitchen and try the door to the Mom Cave. The door sticks, but this time it isn't locked. Taking a deep breath, I open the door. The room is completely dark. I don't turn on the light but whisper instead, "It's okay, Mrs. Simpson, don't be scared. It's just me, Scarlett."

There's no answer at first, but a small circle of light goes on around the tattered old sofa that Mom crashes on sometimes. I blink at the brightness. A gnarled hand draws back from the light switch, pulling a faded quilt up to her neck. Her hair is a halo of silver; the lines in her skin softer and less pronounced.

"Scarlett," Mrs. Simpson says. She puts a finger to her lips. "You won't tell Emory I'm here, will you?"

"Of course not." I step inside. Although I guessed the truth, I can still hardly believe my eyes. I mean, *Mom* of all people is hiding our neighbor away—in her office?

"Your mother has been very kind," Mrs. Simpson says.

"That's good," I say. "Hard to believe, but good—really."

"Won't you sit down?" She gestures to the swivel office chair.

I perch on the edge of the chair. "We made you supper tonight and last night, but you weren't there. My friends brought your cat back too."

She blinks. "Treacle? Treacle's back?"

"Yeah," I say. "He's back. And your nephew came by."

"Oh, Emory." She sighs and *tsks*.

"He said some things, Mrs. Simpson. Things that got me kind of worried."

"What?" She grins widely. "That I'm losing my marbles and need to go to a nut farm?"

I blink in surprise at her language. "Well, I don't think he's right or anything. But yeah...something like that."

"What exactly did he say?"

I take a breath. "He said that you weren't eating. That you forgot to do things because you had…"

"Dementia," she finishes.

"So do you?" I ask, feeling scared of the response.

Mrs. Simpson gives a sad little laugh. "When you get to be my age, your mind is full of everything you've ever done in your life—not to mention regret at things you haven't done. With all that clutter, do you think there's room for things like what day it is and when it's time to go shopping or pay the bills?"

"Maybe not. But people still have to do those things."

"Yes." She nods. "You're right, they do. But that doesn't mean they have to be shut away someplace where people sit around watching television, eating boring food, and waiting for a nurse to help them to the bathroom, does it?"

I purse my lips. "He also told us about your daughter. That she, um…passed away."

She looks at her gnarled fingers but doesn't answer. I press on, knowing this is the key to everything.

"She was the one you wrote the inscription to, right? 'To my little cook.' You made the notebook for her. You cooked things together—you taught her. And then when she grew up, she went on to become a real chef. One of the best, Mr. Kruffs said. You must have been so proud."

A tear forms in the wrinkled corner of her eyes. "Yes, you're right, Scarlett. Right about it all. Marianne was my daughter; my little cook. She was everything to me. You also asked me once about the 'secret ingredient.' Well"—she takes a breath—"it's something that everyone has to find for themselves, the thing that makes life worth living. My daughter was all that to me and more. And now...she's gone."

"I'm so sorry." I reach out and take her hand.

Her grip is surprisingly strong. "Thank you, child."

We sit like that for a few minutes without speaking. I wish I knew the right thing to say, but deep down, I know that there is no "right thing."

She draws a rasping breath. "My nephew means well. And he's right about one thing—my health isn't what it once was. In truth, sometimes it feels as if I'm marking time. I try to keep busy with the house and the cat and the garden. But as for cooking..." Her blue eyes are pools of tears. "For a long time I couldn't face that. All those smells and tastes—all those memories."

"I...I think I understand."

"And then you girls came along. You broke into my home and shook up my life. You brought me those oatmeal bars in the hospital..." She wrinkles her nose. "Mind you, I was *not* a fan of the crystallized violets."

"Oh!"

"But I knew then that my life wasn't quite over. I realized I have things to do before…" She shakes her head. "Anyway, I'm not going to let Emory put me away somewhere, even 'for my own good,' no matter how nice it is, and how much it might make my life easier. Not without a fight."

"And we're going to help you." I squeeze her hand.

"Yes, well." She leans back on the pillow as if the effort is too much. For a second, she winces and rubs a spot on her head just behind her ear.

"Are you okay?" I say, suddenly worried.

"Fine. I get headaches sometimes, that's all."

"Do you want an aspirin? I know where Mom keeps them."

"No, child."

We sit in silence for a few moments. "We cooked him dinner," I say haltingly. "Mr. Kruffs came by while we were making Peter Piper's Pepper Pasta with salad and homemade sauce."

She pulls her hand away, startled. "You cooked for Emory?"

"Um…yeah. He came over while we were waiting for you. We thought feeding him might help."

"And did it?"

"Well…" I hesitate. "He didn't have us arrested when we admitted to starting the fire."

She makes a move like she's going to struggle out of bed. "You told him about causing the fire?" She claps a hand over her mouth.

"Yes," I say quickly. "I mean, we had to. It was the right thing to do."

She sits back, stunned. "The right thing…?"

"Wasn't it?"

Mrs. Simpson looks closely at me. I get the feeling she's seeing me in a new way. "Yes…if you put it like that. I suppose it was."

"We couldn't let him keep thinking it was you when it wasn't! And I hoped…well…that it would be enough."

"But it wasn't, was it?"

"Well, not really. But he did sound really worried about you. In fact"—I lower my voice—"he said he'd call the police if you're not back home by this weekend."

"Pah! The police! That's one thing he won't do. Not while he's in the middle of his campaign."

"That's good," I say. "But maybe you can at least let him know you're okay?"

"Yes," she says with a sigh. "I'll do that. I'm a distraction he doesn't need right now—I know that. And I don't want to be a burden to anyone." Her breathing grows quick and shallow. A knot of anxiety tightens in my chest. She may not be off her rocker, but Mrs. Simpson is really old.

"Don't worry, Mrs. Simpson," I say in a soothing voice. "But is Emory really such a bad person? Gretchen didn't seem to think so."

"No, he's not a bad person." She sinks back into the pillows. "In fact, he's a very good person. He and Marianne were practically best friends growing up. She loved cooking him his favorite desserts for his birthday and at Christmas— Emory was such a serious boy, but his face would just light up when he saw the food." She smiles faintly. "And when I put in the kitchen next door, he arranged everything. We were close once…" She sighs.

"I know the feeling," I mutter.

"I realize Emory just wants to do what's best. And in fact, he may well be right…"

"No, he isn't!" I say. "Because we're going to look after you." I take back her hand. "Me and the Secret Cooking Club. And maybe"—I still can't quite believe it, but it must be true— "Mom too. I mean, she let you come here and hide out."

"Yes, she did."

"And Gretchen knows about these things. You can get an emergency button installed, with a necklace-thingy to call for help if you need it, and have a caregiver come to visit you—even live-in. You could go on like that for a long time. And if someday in the future, you want to go into a nursing home…" I shudder. "Well, that should be your choice."

"Thank you, child," she says. "I admire your spirit. And you've given me a lot to think about. It's good to know that even at my age there are still…possibilities." She stifles a yawn. "And now, if you don't mind, I think we both need to get some rest. It's been quite a day."

"Good night," I say, kissing her on the forehead. I give her hand a squeeze, but she's already asleep.

CHAPTER 35

Finding the Magic

THE NEXT MORNING I WAKE up late, exhausted after a night tossing and turning. I squint against the sunlight and the thoughts bombarding my head. What to do about Mrs. Simpson? Can we make Mr. Kruffs see reason? Has anyone seen my blog? And then I remember I'm supposed to be meeting up with Nick Farr today after school. My insides get jumpy.

I smell breakfast from the top of the stairs. My stomach growls. Mom is already in the kitchen with Kelsie. Mrs. Simpson has cooked a huge breakfast of eggs, bacon, and buttery croissants. Miraculously, my sister's plate is almost clean, and there's not a smear of ketchup in sight.

Mom beams at me as I come into the room. "Scarlett, I see you've found out about my little secret."

I stand there for a second, staring at her. Then I rush over. "Thank you, Mom." I give her a hug—the first one willingly given in a long time.

"Oh, Scarlett!" Mom squeezes me back. She smiles. "And actually—it's no longer a secret. Rosemary called her nephew before breakfast and told him she was here."

I step away, flooded with emotion. Mrs. Simpson gets up from the table, straightens her apron, and takes a plate off the rack for me.

"I can serve myself, Mrs. Simpson," I say. "You eat. This is fabulous."

"No, child," she says. "Sit down. This is my treat."

It's like the kitchen is filled with a warm glow—food and kindness and unlikely friendships. Mom takes a second croissant and, closing her eyes, takes a bite.

"This is divine, Rosemary," she says. "I'd forgotten how good real food tastes. In fact"—she looks at me and smiles—"I'd forgotten a lot of things that are important."

I smile back, blinking to make sure I'm not still asleep and dreaming the whole thing. This can't be real.

"Tell her what you told me," Mrs. Simpson coaxes Mom. "All of it."

Mom takes a long breath. "There are things about my past

that I haven't told you, Scarlett. Things that were painful, and I wanted to forget them."

I stare at her. Mom almost never talks about her past. Across the table, Mrs. Simpson nods encouragingly as though they've practiced this.

"You may not know it, but my grandma used to live with us when I was a girl. She wasn't quite all there after her husband died, but she was kind and she helped look after me when my dad left, and Mom had to go to work."

"Your dad left your mom?" I try to digest this new piece of information. I never knew either of Mom's parents—they both died before I was born. Dad's parents lived a long way away, so we never really saw them either. Because I never had grandparents, I never missed not having them. Or not knowing anything about them.

"My dad ran off with his secretary. I never saw him again." She swallows hard. "At first I blamed Mom—for losing my dad, and then for having to work. She was away just about every night. All she could find was a job as a bartender pouring pints at a bar. I'd wait up sometimes until she came home, smelling of smoke, sweat, and stale beer. I hated it." She takes a long sip of the fresh-brewed coffee.

"But when my grandma came to live with us, everything

changed." She stares off into the distance. "It was like there was magic in the house. She was a wonderful cook, and she told stories, and she played the piano..." Mom drifts off. "It wasn't magic really. It was just...nice."

"It sounds like it," I say encouragingly.

"Then she died."

Mrs. Simpson puts her hand on Mom's arm. "Everyone does, my dear." She gives a long sigh. "But that doesn't mean the magic didn't exist. I know it existed when I was with my daughter, Marianne. It was an everyday kind of magic."

"I don't know." Mom's voice quavers. "Not anymore. I tried to shut it out of my mind for so long. I vowed I wouldn't be like my mom—stuck in some degrading job, never having any money or any freedom."

"Of course, dear," Mrs. Simpson says.

"So when your dad left, Scarlett—just like mine did—I was determined to take control of my life. I started the blog and that grew into something"—she hesitates—"amazing. For the first time, people were paying attention to me. For the first time, I was important."

"No, Mom," I say softly. "You were important before. To me and Kelsie."

"I guess I should have realized that. Instead, I let the blog

take over my life. I became just like my mom. Worse, in fact."
Her eyes glisten with tears as she looks at me. I now see understanding etched in the lines around her eyes. The things she
did and how she made me feel. "Much worse," she says.

"Oh, Mom…" I'm crying too.

She takes my hand and squeezes it. "But then I started to
smell the cooking coming from Rosemary's kitchen. It was as
though the memories were there on the other side of the wall,
trying to find a way to creep through the cracks and crevices. I
was thinking about my mom, my grandma, and my childhood."
She smiles like she's far away. "And the strange thing was that
it didn't seem painful anymore. Just good. And…right."

"I'm glad, Mom."

She shakes her head. "But I didn't want to face up to the way
things were between us—and that it was my fault. And then the
fire happened. I was so proud of you, Scarlett, and so ashamed
of myself." She sighs. "And then Rosemary made that amazing
breakfast… I went into my office to write about what happened.
But instead, I shut down my computer and went next door."

"You did?"

"She did," Rosemary confirms, patting Mom's hand. "We
had a chat and a nice cup of tea." She smiles wryly. "Actually, a
whole pot. She helped me clean up after the fire."

"Really?"

Mom laughs. "Honestly, Scarlett, even a toxic waste dump can get cleaned up if you put your mind to it. Which might be a good project for this weekend. We could tackle your room—together."

"Okay." I smile carefully. "But you're not going to, you know, write about it? Or write about not writing about it?"

She sets her lips determinedly. "I told you the blog was going to take a new direction. I've been thinking about it for a while—ever since the day you brought home those cinnamon scones."

"Really?"

"Really. I've gone back and checked all the analytics, plus my comments and interactions. They all show a definite trend."

"What?" I say, my stomach twisting.

"The bottom line is, there's a strong calling among my followers for me to become an inspirational blogger."

"A what?" I'm not sure I like the sound of that.

"I'm going to focus on *inspiring* other moms and women. I'll be kind of like an online coach for women who are looking to start a business, or change careers, or who simply want a new lease on life. I want to help them to follow their dreams— just like I did."

"Oh." For a second I think she must be joking. But her face is serious.

"Which means, Scarlett, that I'm afraid you're no longer going to have a starring role."

"I... I'm not?"

"No." She smiles. "I'm going to be a whole new mom to you and your sister. I promise."

Something loosens inside my chest, and I feel a flood of relief mixed with another half-remembered feeling...

Hope.

"And Rosemary's going to help me," Mom says. "And we're going to help her—just like you did that night. After all—that's what neighbors do, isn't it?"

· CHAPTER 36 ·

Friends and Followers

I LEAVE FOR SCHOOL IN a daze. It all seems like some kind of dream: Mom's story, her guilt, her "new direction," and the fact that she's actually helping another human being who's in trouble. I don't believe in magic—not the fairy-tale kind, and certainly not "everyday" magic, whatever that is. But I can't deny how much things have changed since Mrs. Simpson came into our lives.

They talked about the details while I was finishing my breakfast. Mrs. Simpson will get a part-time caregiver to look in on her, but Mom and I will help her out too. Mom will speak to Mr. Kruffs and try to get everything squared away with him. How she's going to find time to do all this, I'm not quite sure, but she actually gave me her old phone so we can "keep in touch" if Mrs. Simpson needs anything. And even if Mom really is transformed, she and I still have a lot of issues to figure out. I accept that she's sorry, and I forgive her. But as they say, "The proof is in the pudding." Still, for now, it's a lot more than I ever expected.

The school day goes by quickly, and at the end of the day, my pulse races at the prospect of meeting Nick. I make my way to the library, worried that my knees might turn to jelly at any moment.

Nick is already there with his computer on.

"Hi, Scarlett." He pushes his wavy, brown hair back from his forehead.

"Hi." I try to slow my breathing and sit next to him.

"I see you've got your blog up and running," he says. "I think it's a great idea."

"Well, I did what you said. But I still need to figure out all the different pages, and I'm not sure the layout is quite right—"

He beams at me, and my heart almost stops. "You've already got twelve followers. Not bad for less than a day, don't you think?"

"Twelve?" I lean over and scroll down the screen. The little counter at the bottom that Nick inserted shows twenty-two people have visited my blog, and twelve of them have signed up to follow it.

"It's real, then." My fingers on the keyboard begin to tingle with something like excitement. It strikes me that this is what Mom must feel every time she makes a new connection with a total stranger.

"Yeah," Nick says. "It is." He helps me add the four additional pages: "Yummy Cakes and Bakes," "Healthy Bites for Home," "Home-Cooked Dinners," and "Recipes for Sharing," and add some boxes for uploading photos.

"Now," he says, when all the pages are up. "There are some things we can do to increase your following. Sign you up for some other social media sites and then link everything together. You've got to build your online presence—strike while the iron's hot."

"Okay." I sit there watching him as he goes about setting things up for me. I know I ought to be paying more attention to the stuff he's doing, but instead I'm transfixed by his long fingers typing expertly on the keyboard, and his chocolate-brown eyes as he concentrates on clicking, linking, adding icons, and creating my profile as the "Little Cook" on other sites.

"What password do you want?" He turns to me, and I sit back, startled.

"Oh…" I think for a minute. "How about 'buttercream'?"

"'Buttercream' it is." He types it in. "Speaking of which, are you still okay for cooking on Monday after school?"

"Monday?"

"My mom's cake." He flexes his fingers. "I can't wait to get started on it. I can count on the Secret Cooking Club, can't I?"

"Of course." I smile. "After all, I owe you one."

"Well, I'm happy to accept payment in baked goods." He gives me a sly little smile.

"So it's true then—the way to a boy's heart *is* through his stomach…?"

"Something like that." He holds my gaze for a second.

My insides quietly melt. OMG.

THE SECRET COOKING CLUB

October 10

Thanks to everyone who's signed up to follow my new blog. I look forward to cooking lots of delicious things together.

Last time I told you about my neighbor—she had an accident and was taken to the hospital. I went to her house to feed her cat and found a very old, very special handwritten-recipe book dedicated to "my little cook"—which turned out to be her daughter. So, I thought, "Why not give cooking a try?"

The first thing I made was cinnamon scones. They were so fluffy and spicy and delicious—you just HAVE to try them. Here's the recipe, by the way.

Oh, and be careful with the oven and the knife. You might need a grown-up to help.

Cinnamon Scones

Makes 14 to 16 scones

- 3 cups self-rising flour
- Big pinch of salt
- 7 tablespoons butter
- ¼ cup sugar
- 1 teaspoon ground cinnamon
- 1 cup milk

For the tops

- 5 teaspoons sugar
- ½ teaspoon ground cinnamon

Preheat the oven to 425°F and lightly butter a baking sheet. Sift the flour and salt into a mixing bowl, add the butter, and rub it in with your fingertips until the mixture looks like breadcrumbs. Stir in the sugar and cinnamon, then add the milk, and stir the mixture together quickly using a rubber spatula.

As soon as the mixture comes together into a soft dough, put it onto a lightly floured work surface and divide the dough in half. Try not to handle the dough any more than necessary. Lightly shape each half into a block shape, then very gently roll each half into a rectangle about 9 inches long, 3 inches wide and $3/4$ inch thick. Using a large chef's knife, cut each rectangle from one end to the other into triangles that measure about $2\frac{1}{2}$ inches across the base. Transfer the triangles to the baking sheet.

To make the topping, mix the sugar and cinnamon, and sprinkle the mixture generously over the tops. Put the tray into the hot oven, on a middle to high shelf, and bake for 10 to 12 minutes, until the scones are puffed up and turning golden on top. Place the tray on a wire rack to cool a little.

You can eat them warm or leave them to cool completely, but they are best if you eat them on the same day. My favorite way to eat them is warm, cut in half, spread with a little butter, and sprinkled with leftover cinnamon sugar.

Oh, and definitely don't forget to preheat the oven. It works much better that way.

Thanks for reading this, and I hope you enjoy making the scones. And maybe you can do what my friend and I did—we left them in the cafeteria at school without telling anybody who made them. Just say: "Free samples from the Secret Cooking Club."

Happy baking!

The Little Cook

CHAPTER 37

The Showdown

WHEN I'M FINISHED WRITING, I upload one of Violet's photos of the scones we made. So far, blogging is kind of fun—not as fun as cooking, but I can see why Mom likes doing it. It's a way to connect with people—something that seems a little easier to do on the internet than in real life.

As I look around my bedroom, I think about how much my life has changed since I started the Secret Cooking Club, not to mention a day ago when I sat in the library and actually flirted—*flirted!*—with Nick Farr. And even though he had to leave to go to his soccer practice, knowing that I'll see him again makes all the good things seem real.

Monday afternoon, as I walk home from school, I'm still excited (and only a little nervous) at the prospect of Nick joining the club. I just know we can make his mom an amazing birthday cake. But as I turn on to my street, my good feeling fizzles away. The black Mercedes is parked in front of Mrs. Simpson's house—it's Mr. Kruffs!

I quicken my steps as I head toward the sound of loud voices coming through Mrs. Simpson's open door.

"This is the last straw, Rosemary. I can't go on worrying like this."

"But I phoned you on Friday. You didn't have to come here, and you don't have to worry about me."

"But I do worry—you know that. I need to know you're safe. Now get your things and come with me."

"No, I won't. I'm not going anywhere."

My heart jolts in my chest. Mom said she would take care of Mrs. Simpson and deal with Mr. Kruffs. Where is she?

Then I remember. She had a meeting with Superdrug today over the final packaging of her Mom Survival Kit. And now Mrs. Simpson is all alone to face him!

I march up the steps to the house.

"It's for your own good, you know that! I'm just trying to help. Please come and have a look. It's a lovely place, I swear—"

"What's going on here?" I try to make my voice sound older.

Mrs. Simpson is slumped on her sofa, her nephew pacing the room in front of her. Her face is a mask of defiance.

"You?" Mr. Kruffs gives me a glare that could melt glass. But just then, I have an idea. I reach into my pocket and take out Mom's old phone. Before anyone even moves, I've snapped a photo.

"Yes, me." I smile grimly. "Scarlett."

"What are you doing with that?" He nods at the phone in my hand.

"Just a picture that the 'senior vote' might be interested in," I say. "Since you're acting for your aunt's *own good* like you said."

Rosemary lifts her cane almost like a thumbs-up gesture. "Scarlett," she says. "You always seem to be in the right place at the right time."

"I try." I grin at her.

Mr. Kruffs checks his watch. "This is ludicrous, Rosemary. You know I have to travel out of town tomorrow."

"She's not stopping you," I say, trying not to let my voice squeak with nerves.

"Stay out of this." He waves his hand like I'm a pesky fly.

"But Emory..." Mrs. Simpson's voice gains strength,

"I've been trying to tell you. You don't have to worry about me anymore. I've found people to look after me. New friends. Scarlett and her mother."

"Oh? Friends that set your kitchen on fire? And I don't see any mother—where is she then?" he says. "When I came here just now, you were out wandering in the street. Why did your 'new friends' let you do that?"

"I wasn't out wandering," she protests. "I was coming back from the corner store. I needed more flour—we're baking a cake."

"Baking a cake?" Mr. Kruffs dark eyes look ready to pop. "Since when do you cook again, Rosemary? I thought all that died with Marianne."

She opens her mouth, then closes it again. Her lips begin to quiver.

"That's so cruel!" I blurt out, stepping forward. "Talking about her daughter like that. That's just awful."

"All right, all right." He backs down. "I shouldn't have said that. But *you* don't seem to have a clue why I'm here."

"You're right," I say. "Mrs. Simpson told you to go—so why *are* you still here?"

"Please stop, both of you," Mrs. Simpson says sternly. "This isn't helping."

Mr. Kruffs and I both look at her, then at each other. In an instant, he pulls himself back into politician mode. I swallow hard, trying to think about how Gretchen would act.

"You seem to think I'm some kind of monster," he says to me, his voice quieter, "when really all I want to do is get my aunt somewhere safe. I called in a few favors and found her a place at a fantastic assisted-living home. It's only about fifteen minutes from here. She'll have her own room, with around-the-clock care. There are lots of social events, and even a kitchen where she could cook if she wants. This is her one chance—places like this don't open up very often. I only want her to go over there this evening and have a quick look. If she likes it and then sells the house, she could be settled there for the rest of her life. She wouldn't have to worry about anything ever again."

I breathe out slowly. "She doesn't want to go. She wants to stay here, in her own home. And we're going to look after her. Between Mom and me and my friends, and maybe hiring a caretaker to help out—we can do it. And she's going to look after us too. Kind of like a grandma."

Mrs. Simpson hobbles forward and takes her nephew's arm. "It's true, Emory," she says. "Catch your train tomorrow and don't worry about me. I'll phone you, and you can join us for dinner sometime later this week."

He shakes his head in temporary defeat. "All right, I'll go...for now. But I think you're all living in a fantasyland."

I step aside as he charges out the door and slams it behind him.

It takes me a second to realize I'm shaking. I steady myself against the door frame. Rosemary sinks back on to the sofa like a tired, wounded animal. We look at each other.

"He's awful to you," I gulp.

She closes her eyes and rubs her temples. "He only wants to do the right thing," she says. "But I'm so tired of fighting. Maybe I should just—"

"No, Mrs. Simpson, don't give up. You can't. It's too bad Mom wasn't here. She would have straightened him out."

"You did a pretty good job yourself." She opens her eyes. The fire seems to be relit in them.

"Thanks." I smile. "And don't you worry about a thing. I've got this." I hold up the phone. "Evidence that he's bullying you. He won't want that getting out."

She squeezes my hand. "Keep it if you like, but I don't think you'll need it. Now, where are those friends of yours?"

I check my watch. "They should be here any minute," I

say. "And by the way, that new member I told you about is going to be joining us tonight. His name is Nick. Are we still okay to help him make a cake for his mom?"

"By all means," Mrs. Simpson says, giving me a little wink. "There's no reason why a boy shouldn't make a cake, or benefit from what else you're learning if he's interested. Though in my experience, we'd better start tripling the recipes…"

Right on cue there's a knock at the door. My heart lurches for a moment as I worry that maybe Mr. Kruffs has come back. To my relief, I open the door and find it's the Secret Cooking Club there in force: Violet, Gretchen, and Alison—and standing behind them, Nick Farr. "Hi, Scarlett," he says. "You okay?"

"Yeah," I say. "I am now."

CHAPTER 38

Hundreds
and Thousands

"WOW, THIS PLACE IS AMAZING," Nick says, on entering Rosemary's Kitchen.

"Thank you, young man," Mrs. Simpson says. She smiles at him and then at me, a twinkle in her eye. "Now, I understand that today we will be baking cakes."

"Yeah," Nick says. "It's for my mom. She's turning forty."

"A spring chicken," Mrs. Simpson says.

"Mom went to art school before she had kids. She used to be a painter. I'm thinking we could make a cake with lots of different colored layers. Is that kind of thing possible?"

Mrs. Simpson beams. "I'm glad I bought two extra bags of flour if that's what you want." She waves her cane. "And if you want color, try the bottom cupboard by the oven. I'm sure this young woman"—she points her stick at Violet—"will be happy to help you with the decorating."

Smiling proudly at the compliment from our teacher, Violet goes to get the icing colors.

We mix, color, and bake, mix, color, and bake. Six layers in different flavors and rainbow colors, three separate cakes. A big cake for Nick's mom, a small cake for us, and a big rectangular rainbow cake for school. It's hard work, and even Nick the star soccer player is sweating before long. The first layers come out of the oven to cool, and Mrs. Simpson oversees the decoration assembly line led by Violet and Alison. They've made three different kinds of icing—fondant, royal, and buttercream, and have filled at least a dozen different piping bags to decorate the cakes. Rosemary's Kitchen looks like a cross between an artist's studio and a fancy bakery. I take one set of cake pans to the sink to wash them out.

"Here, let me help with that," Nick says.

"Sure," I say, handing him a cake pan.

"I can't believe how much fun this is." He picks up a sponge and scrubs the pan. "It's kind of like science class and my junior chemistry set all rolled into one."

"It is fun," I say. "And I'm so glad you joined us."

Just then, our sudsy fingers touch under the water,

and my whole body starts to tingle. Nick looks at me, and I blush. The moment is over, but it happened. Me, touching a boy's hand!

Two hours later, our special cakes are finally finished. We cut open our small cake, and everyone marvels at the rainbow layers in vivid colors. And more importantly, it tastes delicious.

Nick has brought his camera, and when we're done sampling our creations, he sets it on the automatic timer. We all cluster behind the table around Mrs. Simpson. The cakes look fantastic—white icing, decorated with rows and swirls of rainbow icing, glitter flower petals, and multicolored sprinkles called "nonpareils."

"Smile!" Nick says. The camera flashes. We're all sticky and messy and happy, and there are sprinkles everywhere—hundreds and thousands of them.

"You girls—and boy—have a real flair for baking," Mrs. Simpson says. It's high praise coming from her, and we all look at each other and smile. The problems of the day seem long banished into the cloudy night outside.

"I'll be back tomorrow to collect the one for school," I say.

"Are you selling it?" Mrs. Simpson asks.

"No," Violet says. "We'll give it away. Free samples from the Secret Cooking Club." She smiles.

"You have a good heart," Mrs. Simpson says. "All of you."

"Thanks," I say. At that moment I feel as though I can do anything.

When I get home that night, I find Mom upstairs in her room. She's sound asleep, and while she's kicked off her shoes on to the floor, she's still dressed in a beige linen suit, slightly wrinkled.

I kiss her forehead, and she stirs in her sleep. "Scarlett?" she murmurs.

"Yes, Mom, it's me."

Her eyes open. "I'm sorry I wasn't downstairs earlier. I was just so tired."

"That's okay. I texted you that I was going to be late too."

"Oh, I should have checked. I guess I'm not very good at being a mom."

"It's okay, Mom." I take her hand and give it a quick squeeze. "How was your meeting with Superdrug?"

"Good, thanks for asking. They liked my ideas for the marketing campaign, and they're going to run with it."

"Great, Mom." I let go of her hand and turn to leave.

"How's Rosemary? Did you see her?"

"Um, she's fine." I go over to the bed and sit on it. "But

Mr. Kruffs came over. He was really angry—a total bully. I tried to help Mrs. Simpson stand up to him, but it was really hard."

Mom props herself up on one elbow and pushes her hair from her face. "I should have been here. Rosemary needs someone to watch over her. But…" She sighs. "I don't even spend enough time with you and your sister. How can I look after Rosemary too?" She breathes out wearily. "I had no business promising her anything really; it might mean I've only gone and made things worse."

"We just need to find someone to look in on her every day. Like a nurse or a caretaker. Gretchen says that's what they did for her grandma."

"But who's going to pay for that? Can Mrs. Simpson afford it?"

"Well, she can pay some of it, I think. But I've thought of another way we might be able to help."

I tell Mom my idea. She listens intently, her face lighting up.

"That's sounds like a really interesting idea, Scarlett." She pauses for a moment, her brain ticking into blogging mode. "I've got a few suggestions if you want to hear them…"

THE SECRET COOKING CLUB

November 15

I can't believe the Secret Cooking Club Online has been up and running for a whole month already! Thanks so much to my 451 friends and followers— you are amazing! Please keep writing in and sending photos of the delicious things you are making. And don't forget—when you leave free samples in your school cafeteria, leave a note with our web address.

Now for a few pieces of news:

First, the countdown to the online bake-a-thon has begun. Only seven days to go! Click below to sign up and enter.

Second, I'm happy to announce that my mom—yes, you heard that right—is helping us in our push for 1,000 followers. She's going to link my blog to hers and publicize us on Twitter, Facebook, and Instagram. She thinks that together we can raise lots of money to help our neighbor, and raise awareness so that other senior citizens can get the care they need.

Third, we helped our newest member make the most AMAZING rainbow layer cake for his mom. She couldn't BELIEVE he could bake something that good. So, go on, everybody, give it a try—you might enjoy it!

I can't believe how much better things have gotten between Mom and me. I finally told her about the Secret Cooking Club, and also that I accidentally started a fire at our neighbor's house. She was surprised—to say the least—especially about the blog. Things were a little tense again, but we got through it. And now it's almost like we're partners—which seems to work for both of us.

And you know what's surprised me the most? Mom can actually cook! For my birthday she made me a two-tiered cake with purple icing, strawberries, and jelly beans on top—and it tasted really delicious. She and our neighbor sometimes spend hours in the kitchen, making real, healthy, home-cooked meals for me and my sister and my friends. And my friends and I do the same for her. We're finally learning how to respect each other, and it feels good—really good. Maybe now that I'm fourteen, I'm finally growing up.

November 16

Guest Post by *Shh...Mom's the Word*

I've never written a guest blog before on a fourteen-year-old's website, and all credit to my daughter for trusting me to do so when I've done little to earn that trust over the last three years. I want to say to the "Little Cook" that I love you and am proud of you. But seriously... Help! My daughter's bake-a-thon is turning my kitchen into a dumpster!

November, 17

Guest Post by the Little Cook on *Shh...Mom's the Word*

You all know who I am—and way more about my life than I want. But now that I've found my own voice, and Mom and I have talked things through, I feel a lot better about myself and Mom. I don't even mind her writing stuff (the good stuff, at least) about me—well, not too much anyway. But if you want the real story, check out my blog.

The best thing that has come out of all this is our neighbor—she's become almost like an adopted grand-mother. We're trying really hard to raise money for people like her—elderly people living alone—so they can all have a few more home comforts. And if possible, we want to help these older people get together to share yummy food and treats and make new friends. Click here for more information on our online bake-a-thon.

If you think this is a great cause, click on the donation link below and show your support.

Oh, and stay tuned for the bake-a-thon. If you're lucky, you'll have a member of the Secret Cooking Club near you to make something delicious. We are dedicated to sharing happiness and friendship through baking. Even if you're (gasp!) a grown-up, we'd still be pleased to have you as a member. Here's that link again...

CHAPTER 39

The Bake-a-thon

OKAY, SO THE BLOG IS doing really well, and I'm enjoying "meeting" so many new people and connecting with them. But as much as the Secret Cooking Club Online is proving to be a success, the bake-a-thon is keeping me awake at night. We're making tons and tons of food—not only for the school cafeteria, but for other schools, and for the hospital, and a few of the old people's homes in the area, and for a couple of lunch clubs set up specially for older people. In other words, it's a big job. The good thing is that it's not just us—there are twelve people at our school who have joined up. I don't know who they all are (because we have anonymous user names) but hardly a day goes by when there's not something delicious left in the cafeteria at lunchtime. Every day, I get from three to ten new followers on the blog.

Mrs. Simpson is an interesting mix of grandmother, drill sergeant, and kind fairy godmother. The one thing she insists on is that the blog doesn't get in the way of the main event—learning how to cook, and sharing what we cook, not just as pictures, but in real life with as many people as possible.

But not everything is going quite so well. For one thing, Mrs. Simpson is getting a lot of headaches, and sometimes she loses her balance and seems to forget things. And Mr. Kruffs is still in the picture, even though he seems to accept that Mrs. Simpson is not going anywhere—for the moment, at least.

As soon as he got back from his trip, he turned up and paid another visit to Mrs. Simpson. He came by her house and caught us with our hands in the cookie jar—or at least the cookie dough (Mrs. Simpson was helping us to make chocolate-covered gingerbread people). And right away, you could tell he wasn't too impressed.

He launched into his usual tirade about how places at the "nice home" don't come up very often, and wasn't Mrs. Simpson tired of having to struggle through every day on her own? He also wasn't very happy when I told him we hadn't had time to look into getting a caregiver yet for his aunt. But then the really bad thing happened.

Mom must have heard the commotion through the wall of the Mom Cave, and she came over to add her opinion. She invited Mr. Kruffs to our house for a cup of coffee and a discussion about Mrs. Simpson's future. And when I got home hours later and came into the kitchen, I couldn't believe it—he was still there!

"Hello, Scarlett," Mom said, giving me a quick hug. "Emory and I were having a nice little talk."

"Oh?" I replied coolly. *Emory?* My eyes fixed on the half-empty bottle of red wine and the remains of a selection of nice cheeses that Mrs. Simpson had bought Mom from a local shop.

"Yes." Mr. Kruffs stood stiffly. "Your mom is a very interesting person."

"Yeah, she is." I couldn't believe it. Is the "new Mom" all some kind of sick joke? Is she suddenly in cahoots with Mrs. Simpson's enemy?

"Oh, not really." Mom blushed. "We were speaking about publicity, that's all. Building a profile and all that. Which I know one or two things about."

"I confess I'm not familiar with your mother's blog," Mr.

Kruffs said. He smiled at her, looking almost boyish. "But she says she'll forgive me."

"Yes, of course." She grinned back and their eyes locked together. Gross. "Especially since I've started taking it in a whole new direction. Right, Scarlett?"

"Yeah."

Mom's already started transitioning her blog from a nasty tell-all rant to an inspirational women's blog. For the "Parenting" section, she's had this new idea where she and I collaborate. It would be a "dialogue" (her word) between a mother and daughter with a view to resolving their differences. At first I laughed and suggested she'd have to come up with a whole new kit for Superdrug—"Mothers and Daughters Together" or some junk like that. Unfortunately, she loved that idea. I guess I'll try to keep an open mind.

"Anyway," Mr. Kruffs said to Mom, "it's been very nice to meet you, Claire. I'll email you about that gallery opening I mentioned."

Claire.

"Oh yes." Mom's face looked rosy and flushed. "Please do."

OMG. All the blog stuff about "The Single Mom's Guide to Dating" and the "way to a man's heart is through his stomach" came rushing back.

Mom is going on a date with Mr. Kruffs!

"Excuse me," I said in a choking voice. "I've got homework."

"Night, Scarlett." Mom kissed me on the cheek. I went upstairs to my room and stared at the glow-in-the-dark stars on the ceiling. At least they have stayed put while everything else is a whirlwind of change.

The day I've been both eagerly awaiting and secretly dreading finally arrives. The day of the online bake-a-thon. Thanks to all of Mom's guest-blogging, tweeting, and other publicity, I've got over eight hundred followers on my social media sites, and just over a quarter of them have signed up for the bake-a-thon. The format is this: Everyone participating will bake something to take to their school, or the hospital, or an assisted-living home, or local lunch club for senior citizens, or just setting up a bake sale on the street somewhere. Everyone is getting sponsors and publicity from local businesses. People donate to an online charity fund to help the elderly.

Of course, all this is happening out in cyberspace and the world in general, so I have very little control over it. But so far, the donations have been coming in at a steady pace. I've had to set up a whole new site linked to my original blog account to accommodate all the photos that members have been sending in for each of our sections: "Yummy Cakes and Bakes," "Healthy Bites at Home," "Home-Cooked Dinners," and "Recipes for Sharing." And as for my own branch of the Secret Cooking Club—well, we've been cooking around the clock. Every spare fridge shelf, table, counter, container, and cupboard is filled with the things we've made. And in a last-minute "if you can't beat 'em, join 'em" move, Mr. Kruffs called Mom and agreed to match whatever funds we raise from the bake-a-thon, in order to help pay for his aunt's caretaker. So now I'm even more fired up to raise as much money as we can.

I'm up and dressed well before the time Gretchen's mom is supposed to come with her car to get all the food from Mrs. Simpson's house. It's a crisp, bright autumn morning, and I can hear the birds singing in the backyard as I go next door to get things ready. I let myself into Mrs. Simpson's house quietly, in case she's still asleep upstairs. I'm surprised to find her sitting in her light-flooded kitchen, the doors to the backyard flung open. On the table in front of her is a steaming cup of tea and one of the fluffy croissants she helped us make. There's also a piece of paper and a pen. As soon as I enter, she folds the paper and tucks it away.

"Scarlett," she says, reaching out her wrinkled hand.

I take it and she grips my fingers. "It's a lovely day for your bake-a-thon."

I look closely at her lined face. Her cheeks have more color in them than usual, and her eyes seem to sparkle, as clear and blue as the sky outside. She looks younger somehow. She's wearing her nicest flowered dress and ivory, knitted cardigan, and her hair is smoothed back in a neat bun at the nape of her neck.

"You look nice, Mrs. Simpson," I say. "Are you expecting company?"

"No, child." She looks at me for a long moment. "Not exactly. But there's magic in the air today. Do you feel it?"

I stand still for a moment—something I haven't done for a while. I listen to the sound of a pigeon cooing from the roof, the wind rustling through the orange and gold leaves. I feel the warmth of the pale sun on my face. Maybe those things are magic, I don't know. But I feel a little bit calmer and ready to face the day ahead.

"Yes, Mrs. Simpson."

She smiles. "I'm so proud of you, Scarlett."

"Thanks." Her praise means the world to me. I lean over and give her a kiss on the cheek.

Just then, the doorbell rings. I go to answer it—it's

Gretchen and Violet. "Hi!" I say, ushering them in. "Right on time."

We go into the kitchen, but Mrs. Simpson is no longer there—I see her outside in the garden, leaning on her stick and looking up at the sky. She gives us a little wave as we empty the fridge and fill Gretchen's mom's car with overflowing baskets, pans, and boxes of food. Alison and Nick are helping to coordinate food pick ups from some of the new members at our school—Susan, Eloise, and Fraser—who have made even more stuff.

Gretchen's mom drives us over to the places that we've prearranged—the hospital where we once took the oatmeal bars to Mrs. Simpson, two assisted-living homes, the city council headquarters, a branch of a local charity that runs lunches for senior citizens, and several local businesses that have agreed to support us. We're left with a big batch of chocolate chip cookies, brownies, and cupcakes to take to school, and I have reason to believe that several more new members of the Secret Cooking Club (who we haven't met yet) will be bringing things too.

We carry everything inside through the back door of the cafeteria—everyone at school pretty much now knows or suspects who's a member of the Secret Cooking Club, and even if they don't, the cafeteria workers are totally on board and helping us. They've even said that club members can use the school cooking facilities (closely supervised, of course).

So by the time all of us make it to our first class (late), it seems things are going well. I somehow manage to make it through the morning, and then it's lunchtime.

As I leave the classroom, I can already hear the noise from down the hall in the cafeteria. Violet and I lock arms and go there together. As soon as I go through the door, I gasp. It's like a cooking flash mob. The tables are covered with baked goods—either the Secret Cooking Club has far more members at school than I know about, or else the cafeteria workers decided to cook their own recipes and desserts. Everyone is standing around talking and laughing, waving trays, not bothering to line up in an orderly fashion. I'm happy to hear the clink of coins in the "pay what you want" collection box we set up.

Then someone throws open the door that leads to the schoolyard outside, and people begin drifting out for an impromptu autumn picnic. It's against school rules to do so, but the teachers don't try to stop us—they carry their plates full of food outside and sit on the benches and grass along with everyone else. Luckily, the day is still bright and sunny with a mostly blue sky and little puffy white clouds.

I grab a tray and work my way forward into the clump of kids in front of the dessert table (I'm way too on edge to tackle any real food). Someone taps me on the shoulder and I turn around. Instantly, the butterflies take flight in my stomach—the way they always do whenever I'm around Nick Farr.

"This is fantastic, Scarlett," he says. His smile is amazing, his eyes shiny.

"Thanks," I say, blushing. "Not that *I* had anything to do with it—but, I'm sure that the 'Little Cook' appreciates your help with the website."

"No problem." He laughs. "And I saw your mom's new post today promoting the bake-a-thon. She really has turned over a new leaf."

"Well…" I roll my eyes. "It's early days."

"Listen…" He leans in closer. "My brother and his wife got me two tickets to see One New Direction—you know, the tribute band? I was wondering…" His voice suddenly falters. "I mean, if you're not too busy…"

"I'd love to go," I practically gasp. "When is it?"

"The Sunday after next. I can email you the details."

"That would be great."

All of a sudden I'm in the middle of the crowd up at the

food table. I feel Nick take my hand and squeeze it, and then we get separated. I look around for him, my hand tingling, but he's gone.

I let the full implications of what just happened wash over me like a warm bath. *Nick Farr* asked me out to a concert. *Nick Farr* likes *me*!

The whole world feels as though it's in slow motion around me. I grab a samosa, a fruit tart, and a chocolate brownie, unaware of all the noise and the people pushing past me. I still feel like I'm flying as I take my plate outside and find Violet, Alison, and Gretchen sitting in a circle on a blanket on the grass. The others reach out their hands, and we all slap high-fives. I sit and take a bite of the fruit tart Alison made—her specialty dish.

"Mmm. Delicious." I close my eyes to savor the taste.

When I open my eyes again, the sky is suddenly dark as a cloud passes over the sun. A few people look up and hold out their hands as the first raindrops start to fall.

CHAPTER 40

The Secret Ingredient

BY THE END OF THE day, I'm exhausted but happy. I managed to sneak out of class for a bathroom break at one point and checked our site on my phone to see how the online bake-a-thon was doing. Hundreds of photographs had been uploaded, and nearly two dozen recipes. Best of all, we'd raised almost $3,000 so far for a charity that helps elderly people, and that's well before all the pledges have been collected.

After school, I log on to the blog and officially declare the bake-a-thon a success. I can't wait to get back home and tell Mom and Mrs. Simpson. Violet stays to help me collect our dishes and baskets. Gretchen and the others go off to collect the dishes we left at other locations. But when Violet and I come out of the school building, I'm surprised to see Mom waiting in her car. We hadn't arranged for her to pick us up. Even though she's now a "whole new mom," she wouldn't have just randomly decided to come and get us. She leans out the window to call to me, and it's then I notice that her cheeks are streaked with tears.

"Mom!" I cry. "What's up? Are you okay? Is Kelsie okay?"

"Yes, yes, we're fine." My sister is in the back of the car playing a Mickey Mouse game on Mom's iPhone. "Get in the car," Mom says. "We need to go to the hospital."

"Hospital?" Violet and I say at the same time. We look at each other, our faces stricken.

"What's happened?" I say to Mom. But in my heart, I've already guessed.

"It's Rosemary," Mom says. "Come on—get in."

Violet and I shove our things in the trunk and climb inside. Mom drives quickly. No one tries to talk over the squeaky voice of Mickey Mouse. As I stare out the window at the traffic and people walking on the sidewalk, Violet reaches over and puts her arm around me. I bury my face in her hair.

We get to the hospital parking lot and find a space. I can't believe that just this morning we were here, worrying about our bake-a-thon of all things, and maybe even feeling a little smug that this time we weren't here to visit anyone. How quickly things change.

Mom half drags Kelsie along by the hand, and Violet and I follow behind. It takes me a second to register that Violet's got a basket of leftover baked goodies over her arm. We enter the lobby, and Mom talks to the receptionist. She tells us to follow the yellow line—we're going to a different ward than last time. We go up in the elevator and keep walking. The yellow line finally stops before a forbidding-looking door: *Intensive Care Unit*.

"But this can't be right," Violet says. "I mean, she was fine. She was…" Her voice trails off, helpless.

Mrs. Simpson was sick. Really sick. And we hadn't even known it.

The setup inside is nearly the same as the other ward we visited: the same busy nurses, the torturous-looking medical machines in the hallway, doorways to tomb-like rooms. There's an awful smell of disinfectant that doesn't quite hide the "something else" underneath. I bite my lip to keep it from quivering.

Mom speaks to one of the nurses. The woman barely looks up from her computer screen. "Are you family?" she asks.

When Mom doesn't answer right away, I step forward. "Yes," I say. "She's my grandma." The words sound completely right.

The woman waves us to a bank of chairs across from the desk. "Please take a seat," she says. "The consultant is on his way to speak to you."

"But can't we see her?" Violet says.

The woman narrows her eyes like she's not used to arguing.

"We'll wait," Mom says.

We all take seats in the uncomfortable molded plastic chairs. The room seems to swirl in front of my eyes. "I…I don't understand," I say.

Mom puts her hand on my arm. "Rosemary collapsed just after lunch. She managed to press the emergency button on that necklace we gave her. I went over right away and found her sprawled on the kitchen floor. She'd been picking herbs— mint, sage, and rosemary—they were all around her. She was unconscious." Mom's voice catches. "Of course, I called an ambulance immediately."

"Yeah…" What can I say?

She opens her purse and takes out a white envelope. "And I found this on the table in her kitchen—right where she fell." Mom's eyes glisten with tears. "It's got your name on it."

My hand trembles as I take the envelope. I stare down

at the writing, the loopy letters of my name swimming before my eyes.

"She wrote you a letter," Violet says. "Open it."

But I hesitate a second too long. A man in a white lab coat comes into the waiting area. He looks at his clipboard and then at Mom. "Claire Cooper?" he says.

I shove the letter in the pocket of my sweater.

"Yes." Mom stands up nervously. "Kelsie, switch that thing off." She reaches for the iPhone.

"You're Mrs. Simpson's family?" the doctor asks.

"Yes." This time Mom doesn't pause.

"Well, I'm sorry to have to tell you that the news isn't good. Mrs. Simpson came in for some tests last week. She'd been having headaches and feeling weak, as I expect you knew. She knew her condition was getting worse."

"But she didn't tell us any of this," I blurt out. "I mean, I know she had some headaches, but doesn't everyone?"

The consultant nods. "It was quite sudden as these things go. The blood pressure in her brain has been steadily rising. And today she had a major stroke." He takes out a folder from under the top sheets of the clipboard. He shuffles a few papers and then hands Mom a photograph. I gaze over her shoulder. It's a grainy black-and-white scan of a skull.

"You can see the clot here—this dark mass." The doctor points to a spot on the photo. "And now she's slipped into a coma. I'm afraid she's already beyond our reach."

I look at him in disbelief. "But, I don't understand. You mean she's…?"

"Can we see her?" Mom asks.

"Of course, this way."

My legs are unsteady as I stand to follow the consultant. This time it's my turn to grip Violet's hand for dear life. Mom walks next to us, her jaw set grimly. Kelsie shrinks behind her.

As we begin heading down the hall, there's a pounding on the door to the ward, and I hear a man's loud voice. "Let me in, please. Someone let me in."

The nurse at the desk looks annoyed as she buzzes the door. A whirlwind of a man in a black suit marches inside.

"Emory," Mom says in a choking voice. "You're just in time. We're going in to see her."

Seeing Mom seems to calm him a little. He comes over to her and kisses her on the cheek. "I'm so glad you're here," he says, ruffling Kelsie's hair. He glances at me and Violet. "All of you." The sadness in his eyes is genuine.

I look at the floor, unable to answer him. The doctor clears his throat. I lead the solemn procession behind him down the hall.

As we walk, I force myself to look inside a few of the open doors to prepare myself for the worst. Just like last time, there are televisions blaring loudly and shrunken patients lying with tubes sticking out in all directions. I begin to feel dizzy.

The doctor directs us to a single room at the end of the hallway. I pause at the door and look inside. Mrs. Simpson's frame is small and frail in the center of the bed. Her skin is pale, her breathing even. She looks almost serene. The only tube coming from her is from a little finger cuff that leads to a quietly bleeping monitor.

At that moment, I lose it. I rush away from the room and a few yards back down the hallway, leaning against the wall and gasping for breath. The tears rise like a tidal wave inside me. The light blurs to dark in front of my eyes.

A hand grasps my arm to steady me. I blink and find it's Emory Kruffs standing there.

"Scarlett..." he says quietly.

"You were right," I say with a hiccuppy sob. "She should have been in a home with nurses to look after her around the clock. I should have listened—convinced her. If she'd gone to the nice home like you wanted her to, then maybe this wouldn't have happened."

He gives me a kindly smile and shakes his head. "No,

Scarlett," he says. "I think *you* were right all along. She was old and ill—even I didn't know quite how ill—and this would have happened anyway. At least she was able to spend her last days where she wanted to be: at home. She was able to pass her gifts on to you and your friends, and that meant a lot to her." His eyes fill with tears. "I'm glad that, in the end, she stayed where she was, surrounded by her memories, and"—he squeezes my hand—"by people she loved."

I nod solemnly. In that moment, we seem to reach a kind of understanding. Maybe even a truce.

"Come on." He gently tugs my arm. "It's time to say goodbye."

I allow myself to be led back down the hall and into the room. Violet and Mom are seated there on either side of Mrs. Simpson, each holding one of her hands. Kelsie is standing behind Mom, her face almost hidden behind Mom's hair. Violet isn't crying, but her head is bowed. I remember how she was there with her mom at the…end.

She looks up when I enter. I can see the pain there in her purple-blue eyes. "She looks very peaceful," Violet says, trying to smile. "You know, like they say—on her way to a better place and all that."

I shake my head. Wherever Mrs. Simpson has gone, it can't be better than her lovely kitchen.

"I'm so sorry, Scarlett," Mom says. And I can tell immediately she means more than just about Mrs. Simpson.

"No, Mom, it's okay." My voice is remarkably steady. "Um, do you mind if I sit with her for a minute with Violet?"

"Of course, go ahead. I'll be just outside." Mom stands and shifts places with me in the small room. As she ushers Kelsie out of the room, Emory Kruffs takes Mom's hand and they walk out together.

"Mrs. Simpson," I say in a whisper. "Rosemary?"

There's no response other than the breathing. I grasp her wrinkled, arthritic hand. It's cool and slightly clammy. I look over at Violet. She's set the basket she brought with her on the extra visitor's chair.

I let go of Mrs. Simpson's hand for a second and stand. "We brought you something."

I go over to the basket and remove the cloth. I feel like Little Red Riding Hood, except this time I know full well that the wolf is already at the door.

"We've got scones, and a few oatmeal bars, and chocolate-covered gingerbread people." I smile through my tears. "I know you like those." I take the basket back to the bedside. I hold up one of the ginger cookies under Mrs. Simpson's nose. The delightful smell seems to fill the room as if they were just out of the oven. Cinnamon, sugar, corn syrup, spicy ginger. And something else is there too, underneath it all. I suddenly remember the letter that Mom found. I hand the cookie to Violet and fumble in my pocket.

I open the envelope and unfold the paper. It's only a few lines, written in Mrs. Simpson's handwriting. I read it out loud in a soft voice:

My dear Scarlett,

I'm sorry if I didn't tell you just how short my time with you was going to be. But I thought it was probably better that way. I haven't known you very long, but I know you already possess everything you need to become the young woman that you want to be.

The recipe book is yours, and I hope you will keep it always and remember the times we had and all that we shared. Please don't be sad about me, but live your life to the fullest, and I'll be with you always. And as for the secret ingredient—you only have to look inside yourself to find it. And believe...

Love always,
Rosemary Simpson

Tears roll down my cheeks as I finish the last line. Violet begins to sob softly. And just behind me, I'm aware of three other people who have crowded into the room—Gretchen, Alison, and Nick. It's only fitting that all the Secret Cooking Club should come here at the end, to say thank you to her for what she brought into our lives.

One by one, my friends all touch Mrs. Simpson's hand to say goodbye before going out of the room, leaving her in peace. Violet lingers at the door for a second before joining the others.

And then there's just me.

All of a sudden, I feel Mrs. Simpson's hand underneath mine give a little jerk. Immediately I sit forward, hope flickering for an instant. Her eyes are still closed, but her lips move slightly and a word comes out of her mouth: "Marianne."

Her hand grips mine more tightly for a second, and something like a smile plays over her lips. The heart rate monitor begins to drone a flat, steady tone.

She's gone.

CHAPTER 41

Epilogue

THE FUNERAL OF ROSEMARY SIMPSON is held on a gray Friday afternoon. In attendance with me are Mom, Emory Kruffs, my sister, Violet, Gretchen, Alison, Nick, and about a hundred other members of the Secret Cooking Club who came from all around to meet up, celebrate the life of our teacher, and bring lots of delicious food that would feed an army. The occasion draws such a crowd that the local newspaper sends a photographer, and the head of the charity for senior citizens gives a speech praising our charity bake-a-thon. Many more people are present, not so much in spirit, as in cyberspace.

Mrs. Simpson is buried under a shady tree in a corner of the graveyard, next to her daughter and her long-departed husband. I cry at the funeral—of course I do. But at the same time, I feel a strange sense of calm. I know that Mrs. Simpson's with her daughter now—her "little cook"—and that she's at peace. I know the magic is real. And as for me, whatever happens, I can handle it.

I mean, I've already had to come to terms with the fact that Mom seems pretty serious about Emory Kruffs, and there's been talk of knocking our two houses into one (with Mrs. Simpson's fabulous kitchen staying put, of course). Emory's actually okay, now that I'm getting to know him. Believe it or not, he and I have watched a couple of cooking shows together when he's over at our house. He told me a secret too—that when he has time, he might want me to teach him how to cook so he can make something special for Mom. So the Secret Cooking Club might be getting its first real "celebrity" member—or, at least, our first elected official.

But the one thing that does rattle me is when Nick Farr looks for me after the service, offers his condolences…and then reminds me about our "date" in two days to see the concert.

In other words, life goes on.

The evening after the funeral, I sit at my desk with Treacle curled up on my lap. At least so far, he seems content in his new home here with us. I finish typing in one of Mrs. Simpson's special recipes and close the little notebook. I press the button on my new computer to publish it on the blog—sharing what she left behind with all our friends and followers. Beside me is a plate of deliciously fresh miniature butter pastries that Gretchen and Alison made, decorated by Violet with chocolate swirls and gold sparkles on top. I also have a steaming cup of hot chocolate topped with a sprinkling of cinnamon that Mom brought up to my room. I breathe in deeply, savoring the aromas and flavors.

A dash of friendship, a pinch of secrets, a cup of laughter, and a dollop of tears.

And then there's the secret ingredient that's always there—something we have to find within ourselves.

Maybe you've guessed it already.

It's really not all that secret.

That's right...

Love.

Acknowledgments

This book is dedicated to Eve, Rose, and Grace. I love you more than chocolate caramels. I'd like to thank the judges of the *Times*/Chicken House Children's Fiction Competition 2015 for choosing this book as the winner, and all the lovely people at Chicken House, for making the dream a reality. I'd also like to thank my parents, my partner Ian, and my writing group: Lucy, Ronan, Chris, Francisco, and Dave, for your support and belief. Finally, I'd like to say thank you to all my readers—you are the secret ingredient who truly bring a book to life!

About the Author

Laurel Remington works as a lawyer for a renewable energy company that builds wind farms. She lives in the UK with her three girls.

DON'T MISS THE NEXT INSTALLMENT
OF THE SECRET COOKING CLUB

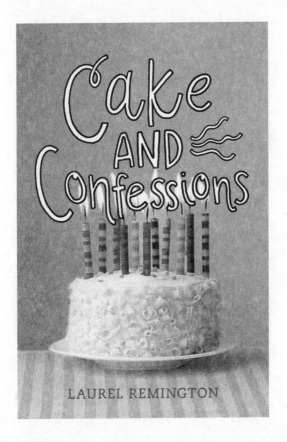

A heartwarming story of friendship, family,
and finding out the things that truly matter.